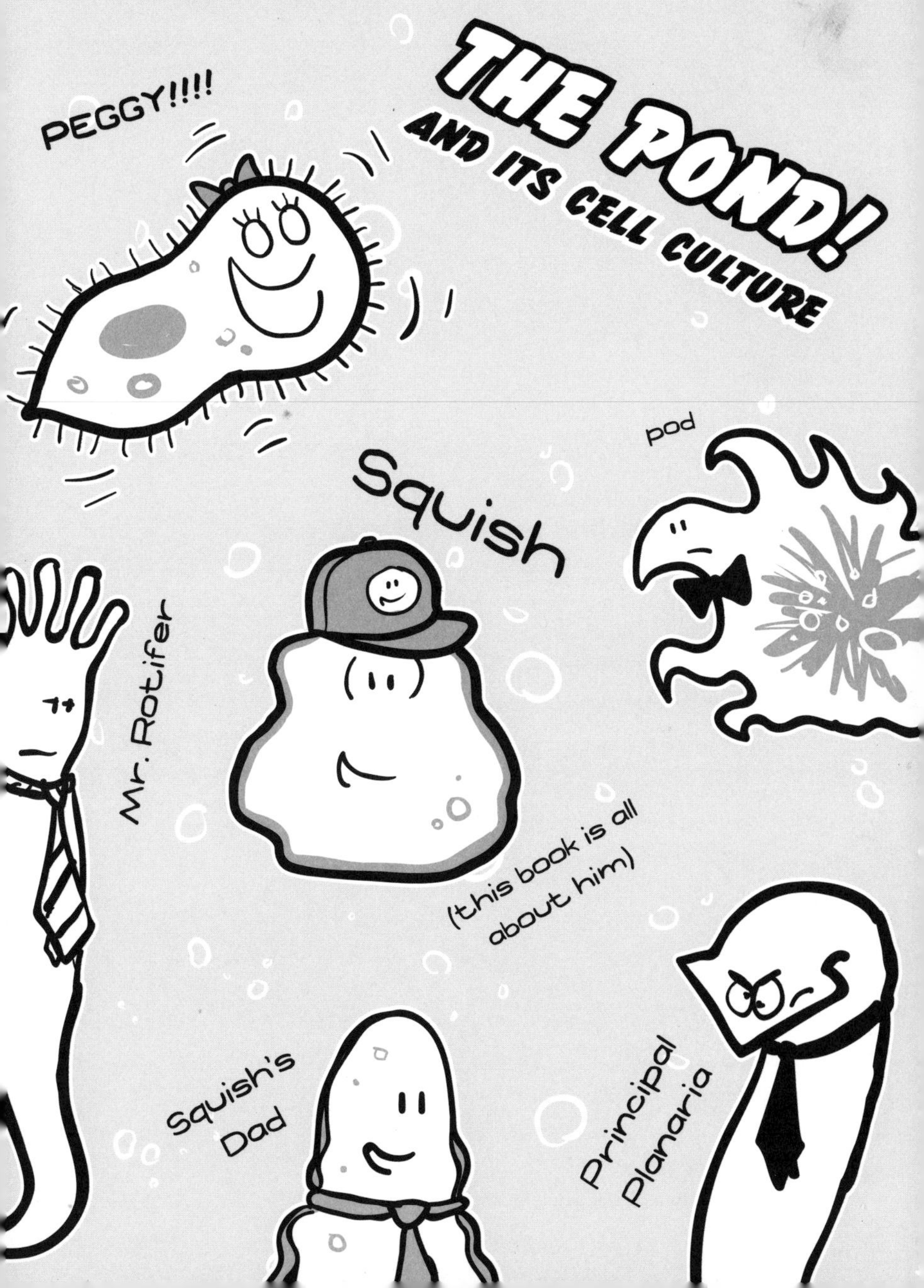
THE POND!
AND ITS CELL CULTURE
PEGGY!!!!
Squish
pod
Mr. Rotifer
(this book is all about him)
Squish's Dad
Principal Planaria

Read ALL the SQUISH books!

#1 SQUISH: Super Amoeba
#2 SQUISH: Brave New Pond
#3 SQUISH: The Power of the Parasite
#4 SQUISH: Captain Disaster
#5 SQUISH: Game On!
#6 SQUISH: Fear the Amoeba
#7 SQUISH: Deadly Disease of Doom

squish
DEADLY DISEASE OF DOOM

BY JENNIFER L. HOLM & MATTHEW HOLM

RANDOM HOUSE  NEW YORK

Published in the United States by Random House Children's Books, a division of Penguin Random House LLC, New York.

Random House and the colophon are registered trademarks of Penguin Random House LLC.

Visit us on the Web! randomhousekids.com

Educators and librarians, for a variety of teaching tools, visit us at RHTeachersLibrarians.com

Library of Congress Cataloging-in-Publication Data
Holm, Jennifer L.
Deadly disease of doom / by Jennifer L. Holm and Matthew Holm. — First edition.
p. cm. — (Squish ; #7)
Summary: When Squish, a meek amoeba who loves the comic book exploits of his favorite hero, "Super Amoeba," starts feeling sick, he worries he has caught a deadly illness.
ISBN 978-0-307-98305-3 (trade) — ISBN 978-0-307-98306-0 (lib. bdg.) — ISBN 978-0-307-98307-7 (ebook)
1. Graphic novels. [1. Graphic novels. 2. Amoeba—Fiction. 3. Sick—Fiction. 4. Superheroes—Fiction. 5. Cartoons and comics—Fiction.]
I. Holm, Matthew. II. Title.
PZ7.7.H65De 2015 741.5'973—dc23 2015000928

MANUFACTURED IN MALAYSIA 10 9 8 7 6 5 4 3 2 1
First Edition

Random House Children's Books supports the First Amendment and celebrates the right to read.

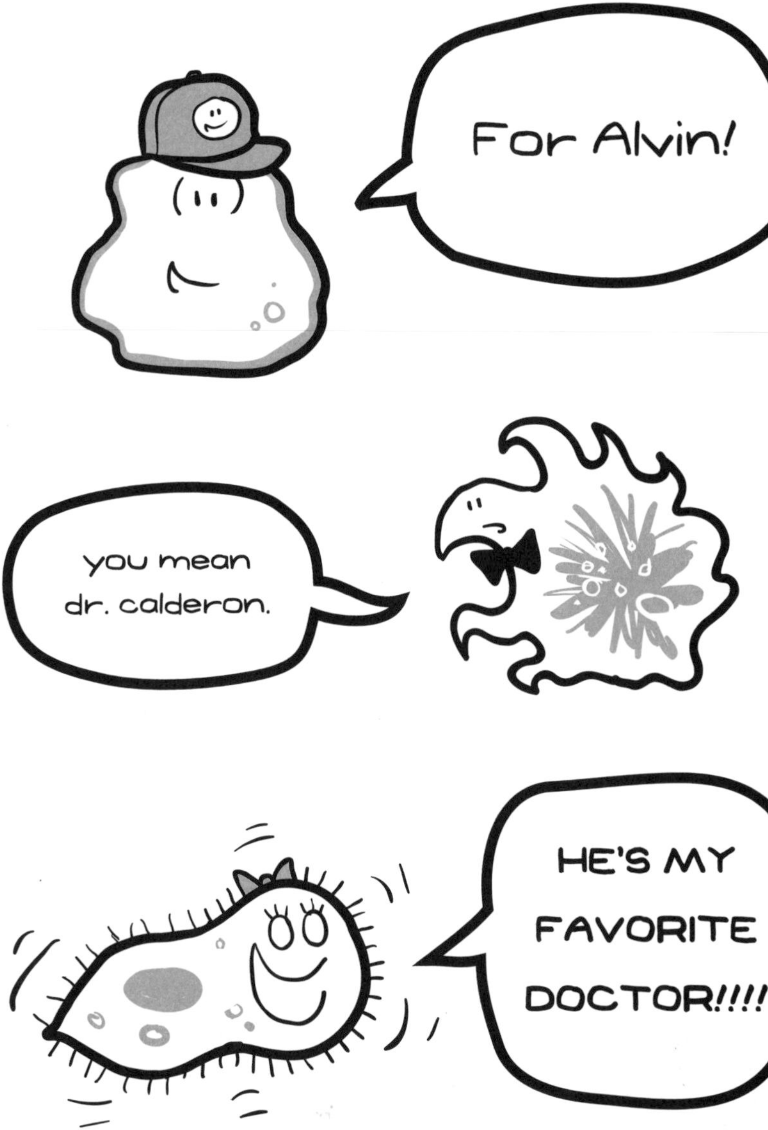
For Alvin!
you mean dr. calderon.
HE'S MY FAVORITE DOCTOR!!!!

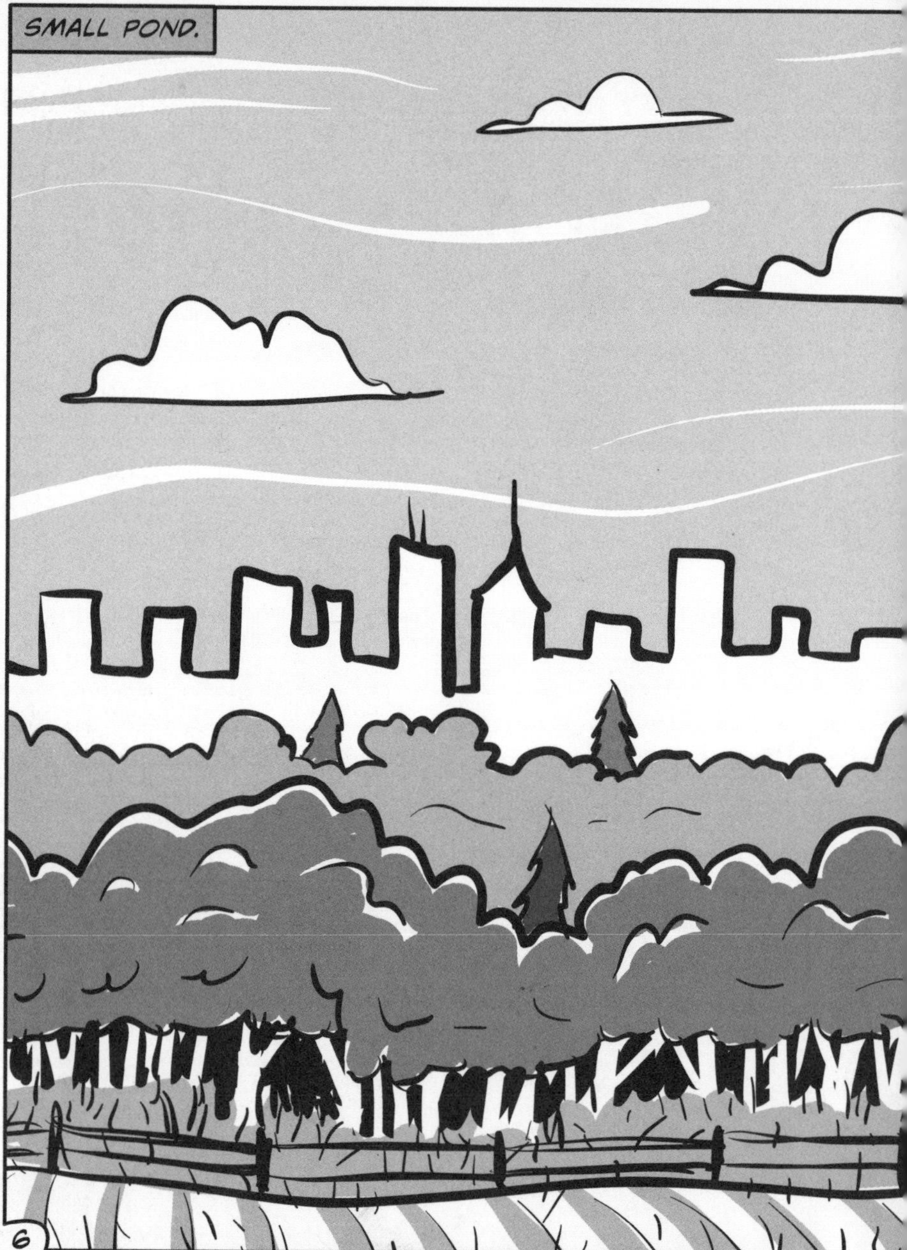
SMALL POND.

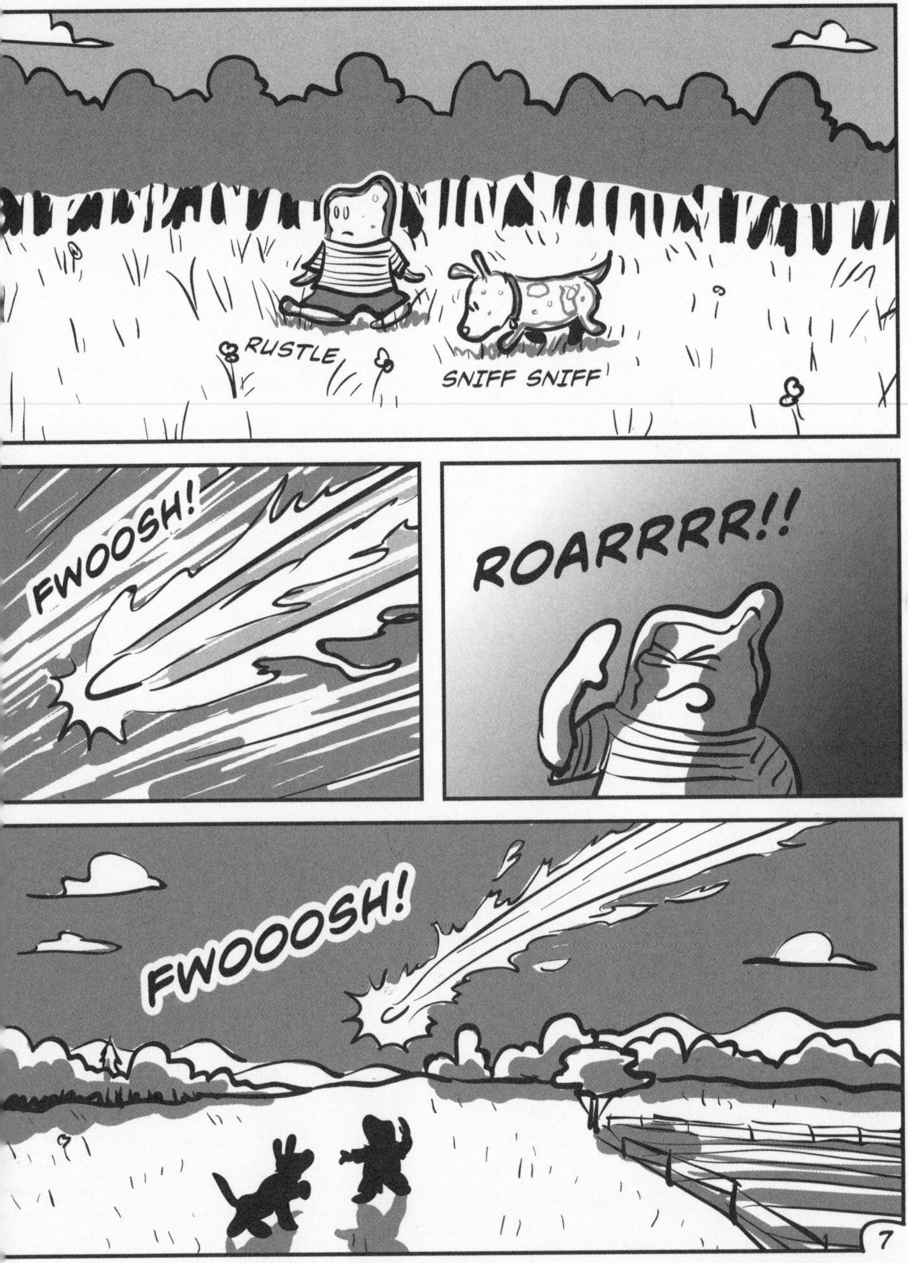
RUSTLE
SNIFF SNIFF
FWOOSH!
ROARRRR!!
FWOOOSH!

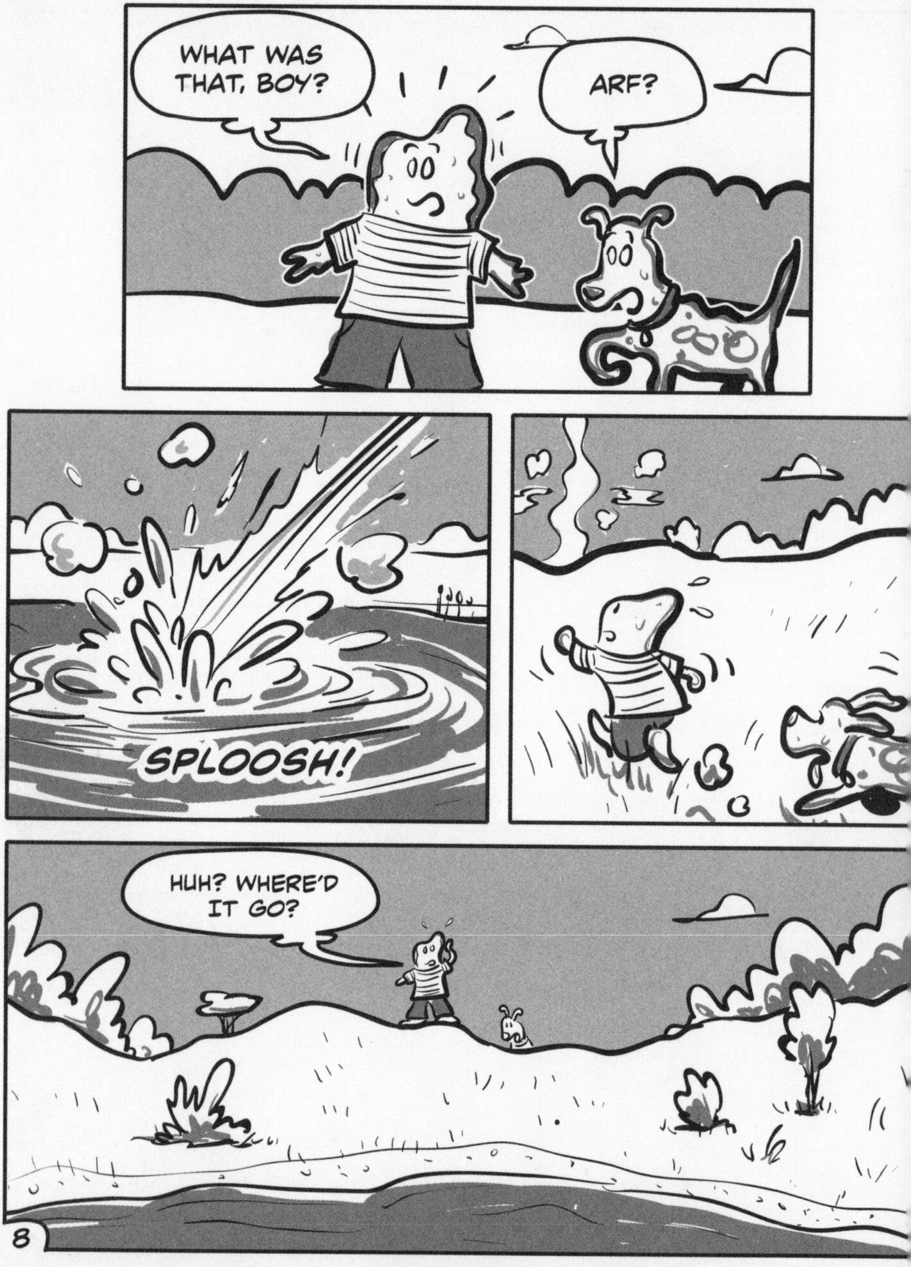
WHAT WAS THAT, BOY?
ARF?
SPLOOSH!
HUH? WHERE'D IT GO?

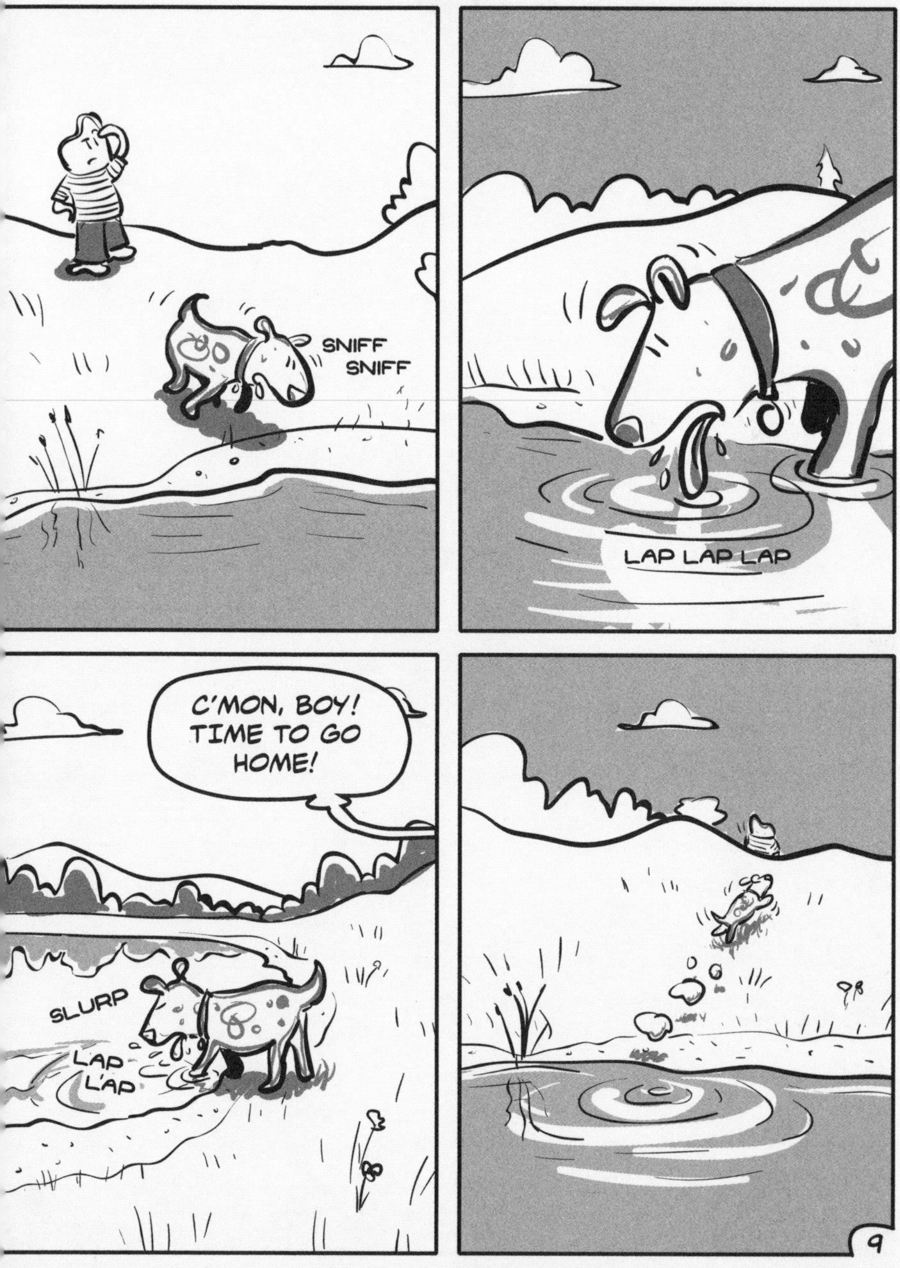

SNIFF SNIFF
LAP LAP LAP
C'MON, BOY! TIME TO GO HOME!
SLURP
LAP LAP

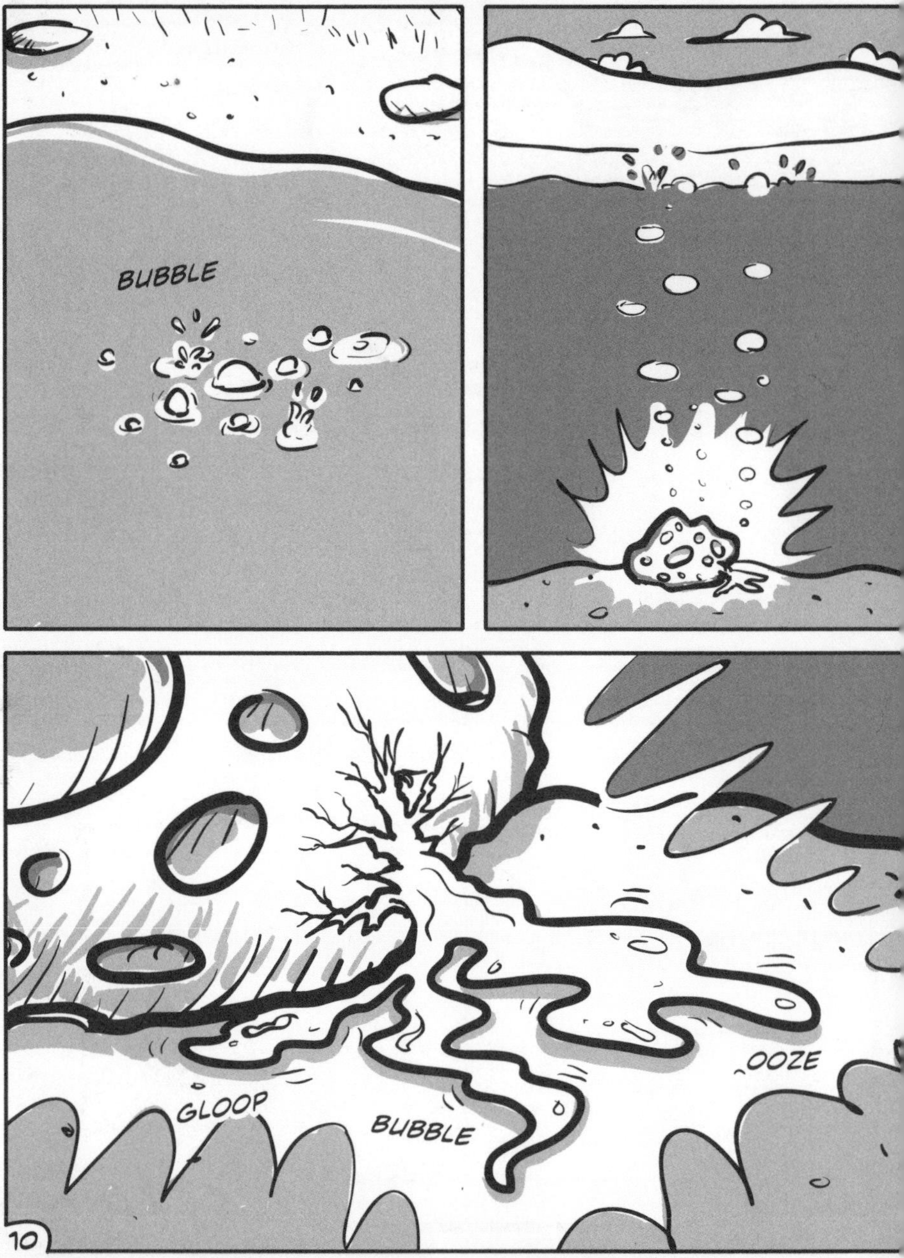
BUBBLE
GLOOP
BUBBLE
OOZE

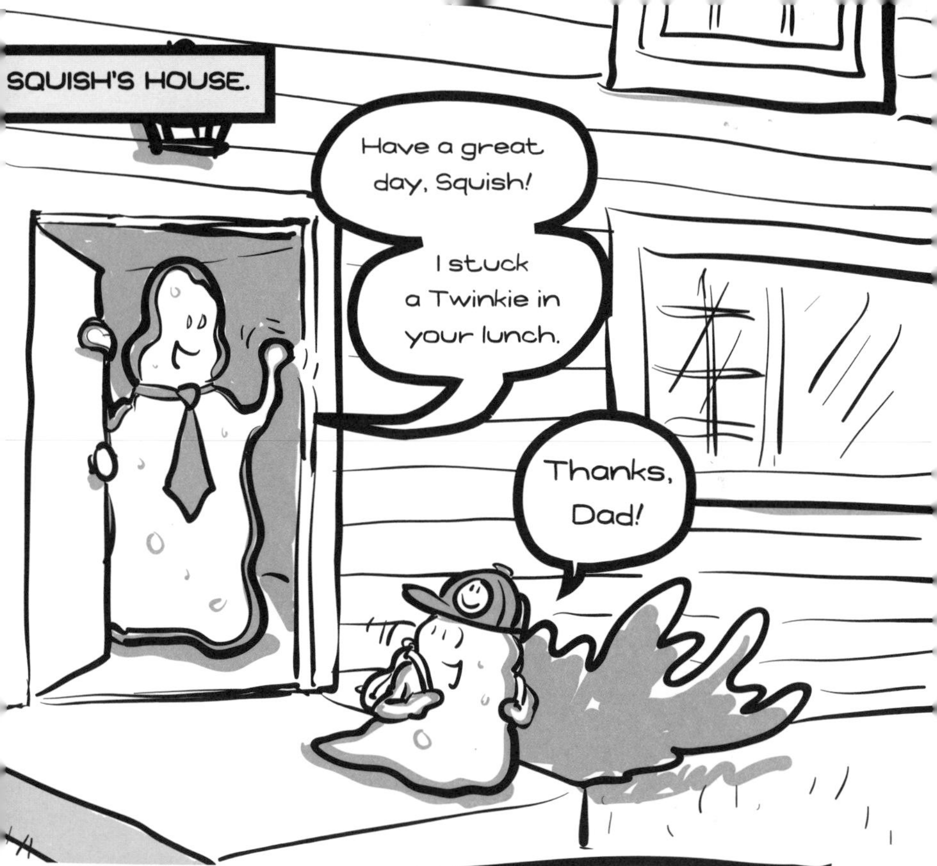
SQUISH'S HOUSE.
Have a great day, Squish!
I stuck a Twinkie in your lunch.
Thanks, Dad!

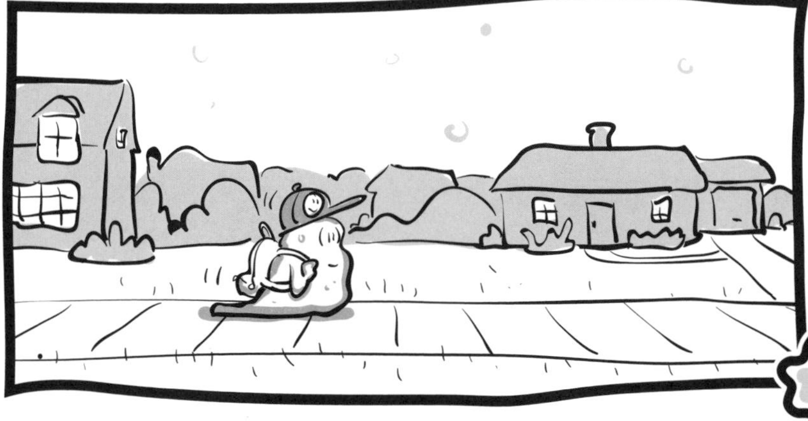

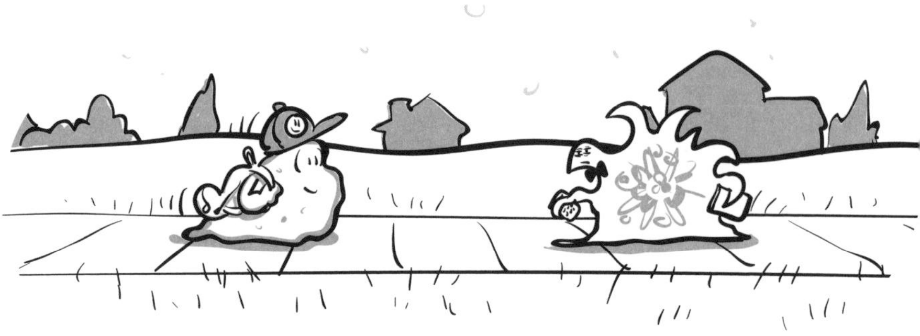

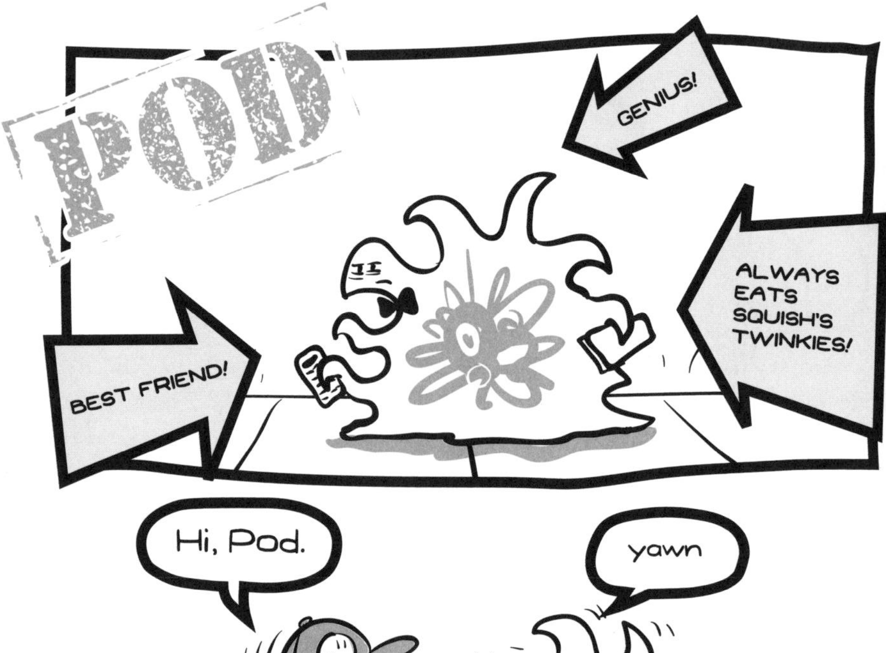
POD
GENIUS!
BEST FRIEND!
ALWAYS EATS SQUISH'S TWINKIES!

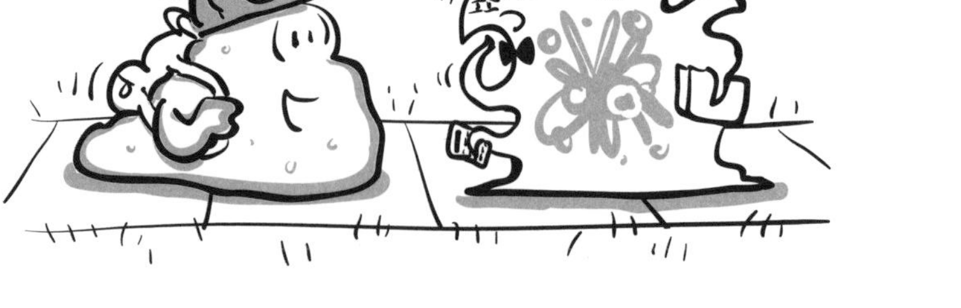
Hi, Pod.
yawn

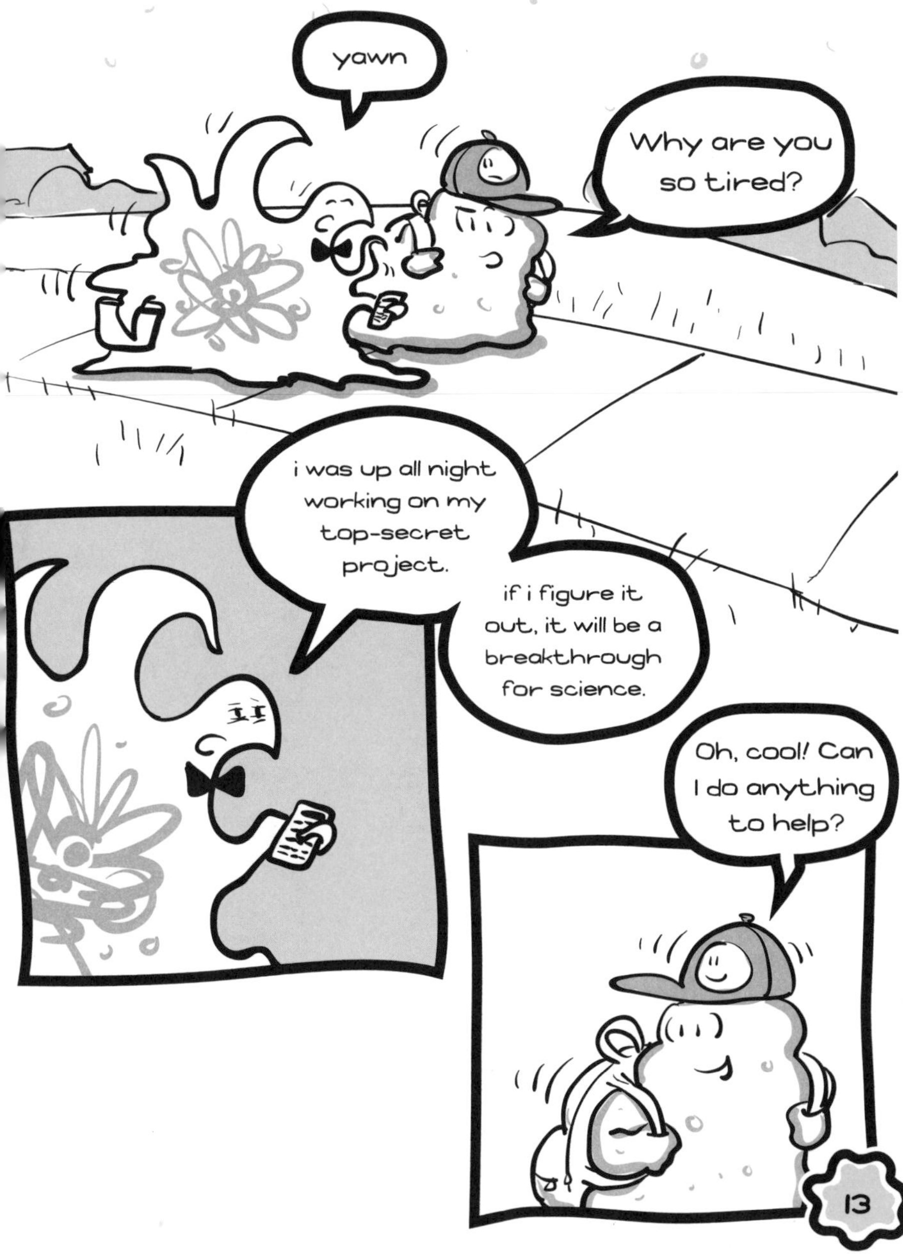
yawn
Why are you so tired?
i was up all night working on my top-secret project.
if i figure it out, it will be a breakthrough for science.
Oh, cool! Can I do anything to help?

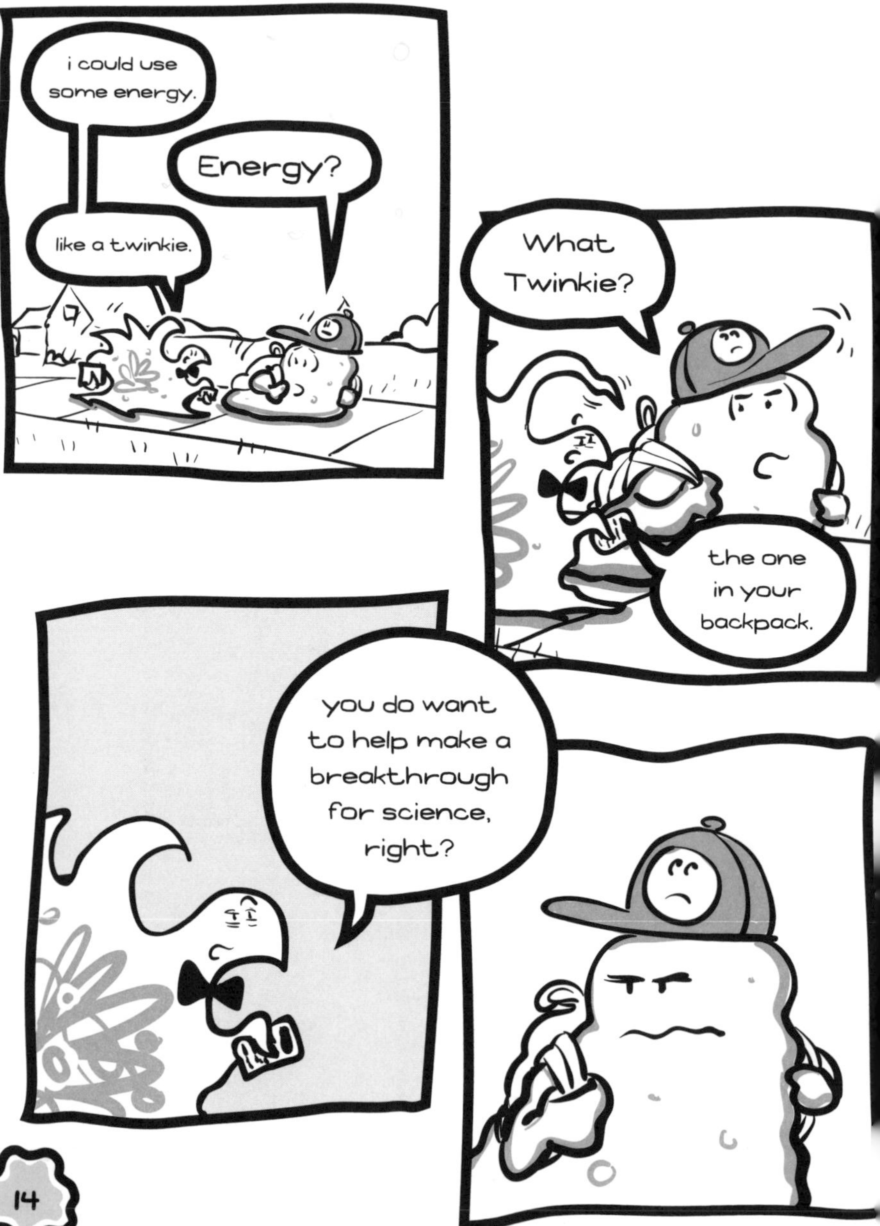
i could use some energy.
Energy?
like a twinkie.
What Twinkie?
the one in your backpack.
you do want to help make a breakthrough for science, right?

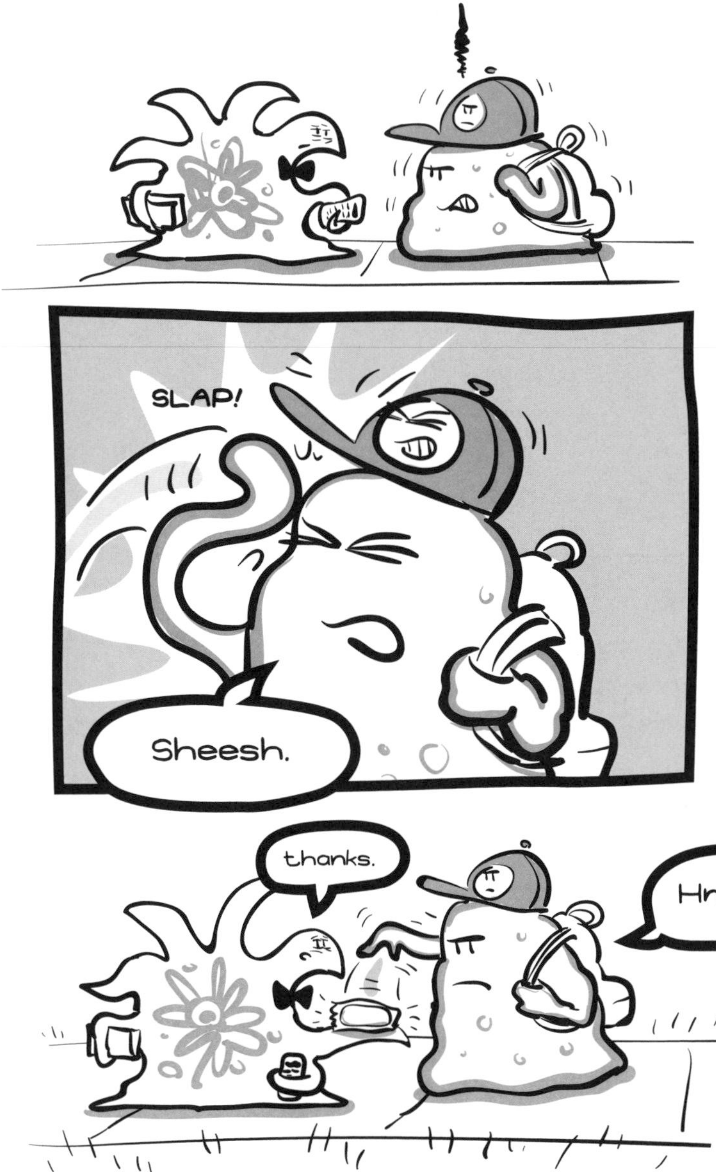
SLAP!
Sheesh.
thanks.
Hmph.

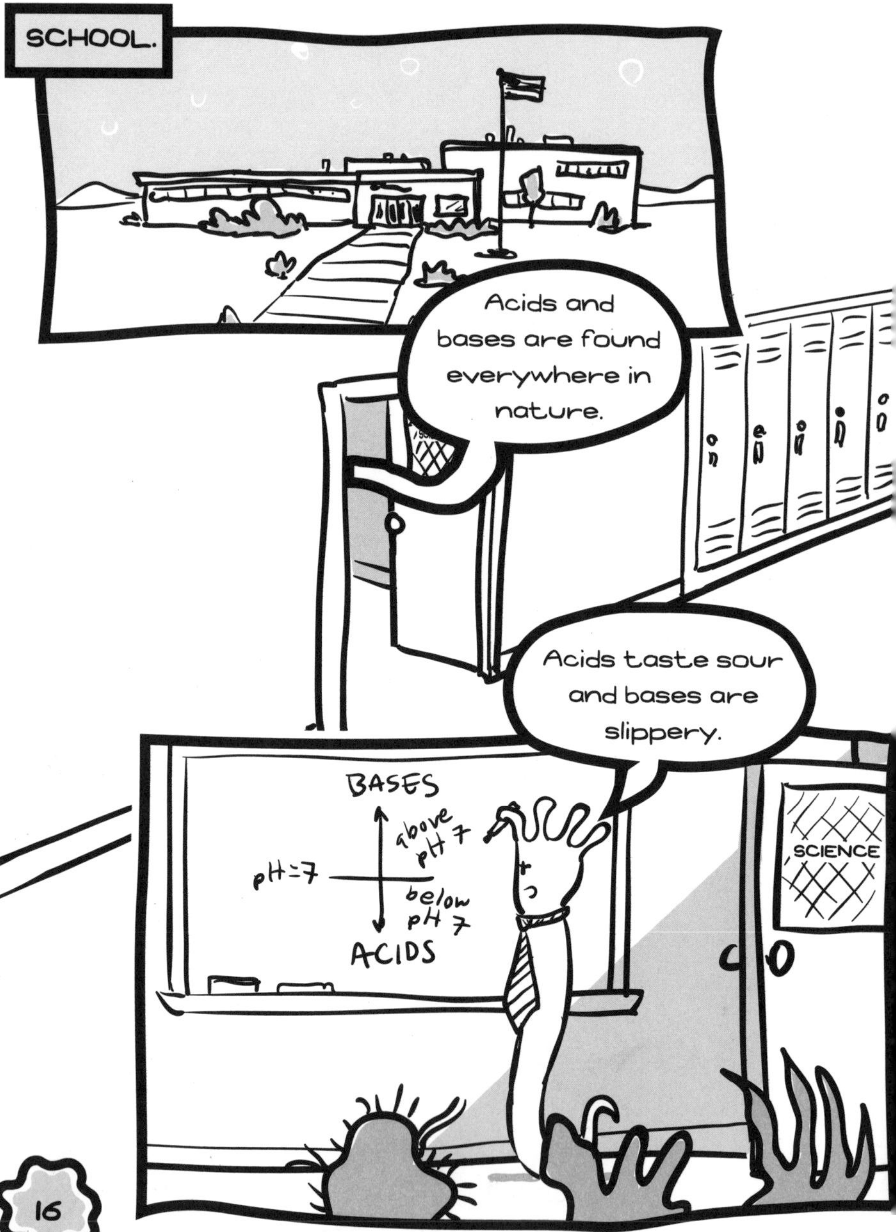
SCHOOL.
Acids and bases are found everywhere in nature.
Acids taste sour and bases are slippery.
BASES
above pH 7
pH=7
below pH 7
ACIDS
SCIENCE

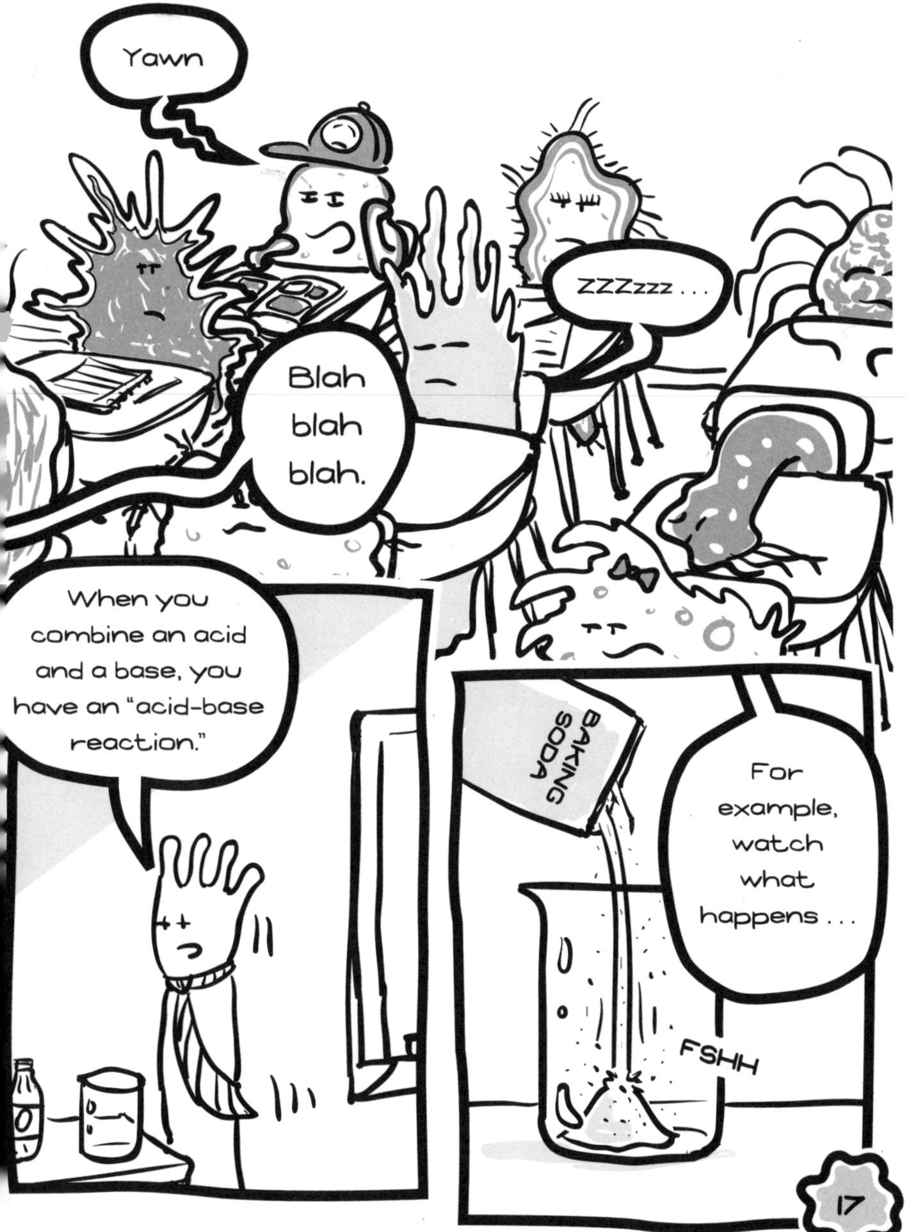
Yawn
ZZZzzz . . .
Blah blah blah.
When you combine an acid and a base, you have an "acid-base reaction."
BAKING SODA
For example, watch what happens . . .
FSHH

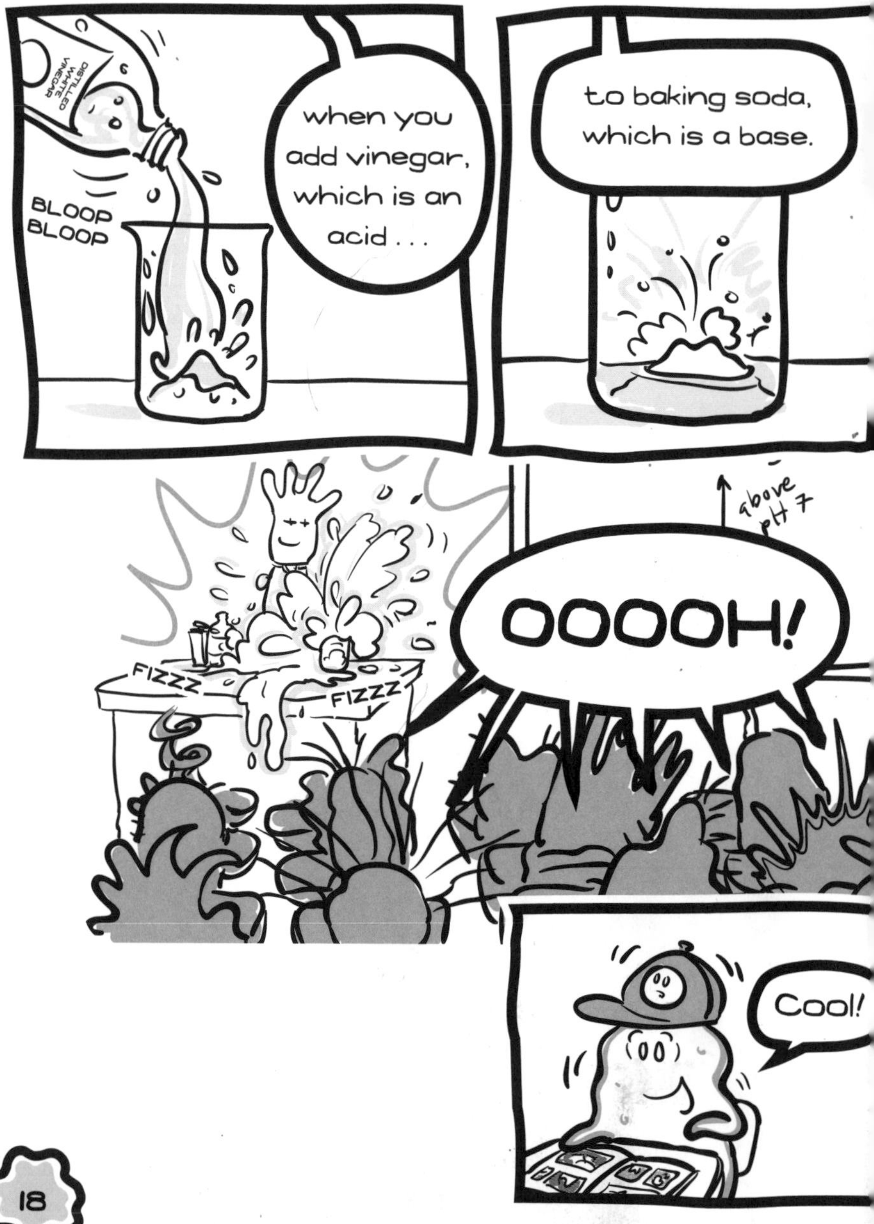
DISTILLED WHITE VINEGAR
BLOOP BLOOP
when you add vinegar, which is an acid . . .
to baking soda, which is a base.
FIZZZ
FIZZZ
above pH 7
OOOOH!
Cool!

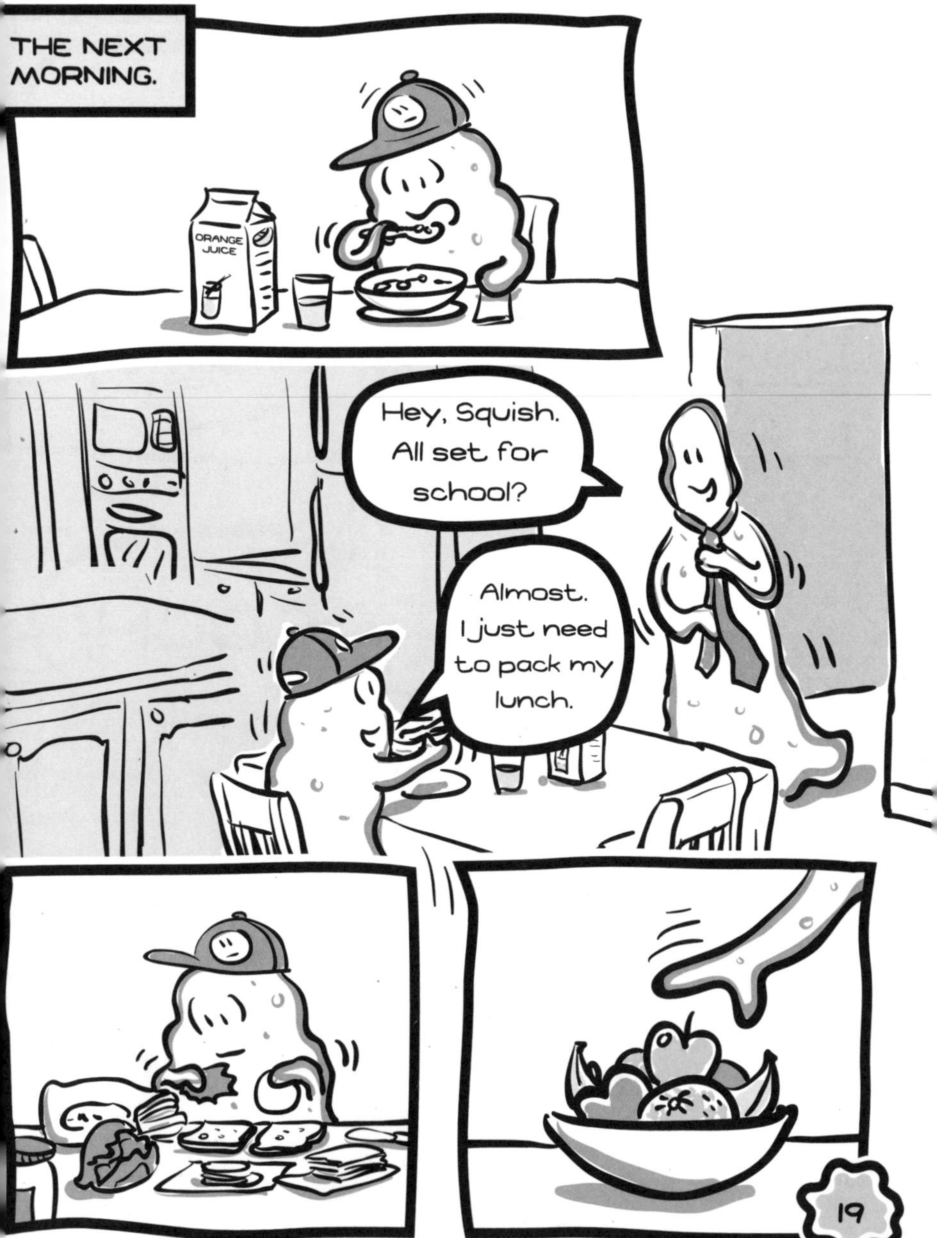
THE NEXT MORNING.
ORANGE JUICE
Hey, Squish. All set for school?
Almost. I just need to pack my lunch.

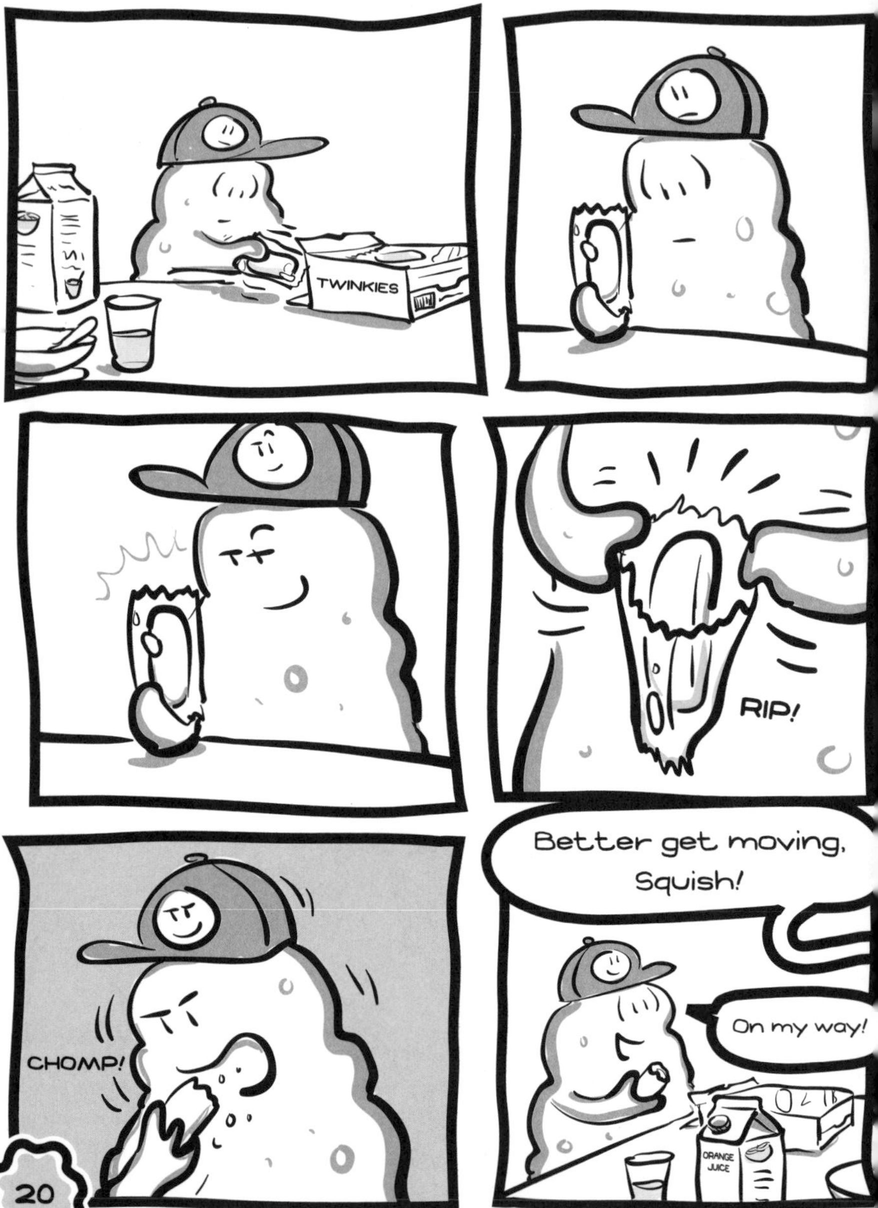
TWINKIES
RIP!
CHOMP!
Better get moving, Squish!
On my way!
ORANGE JUICE

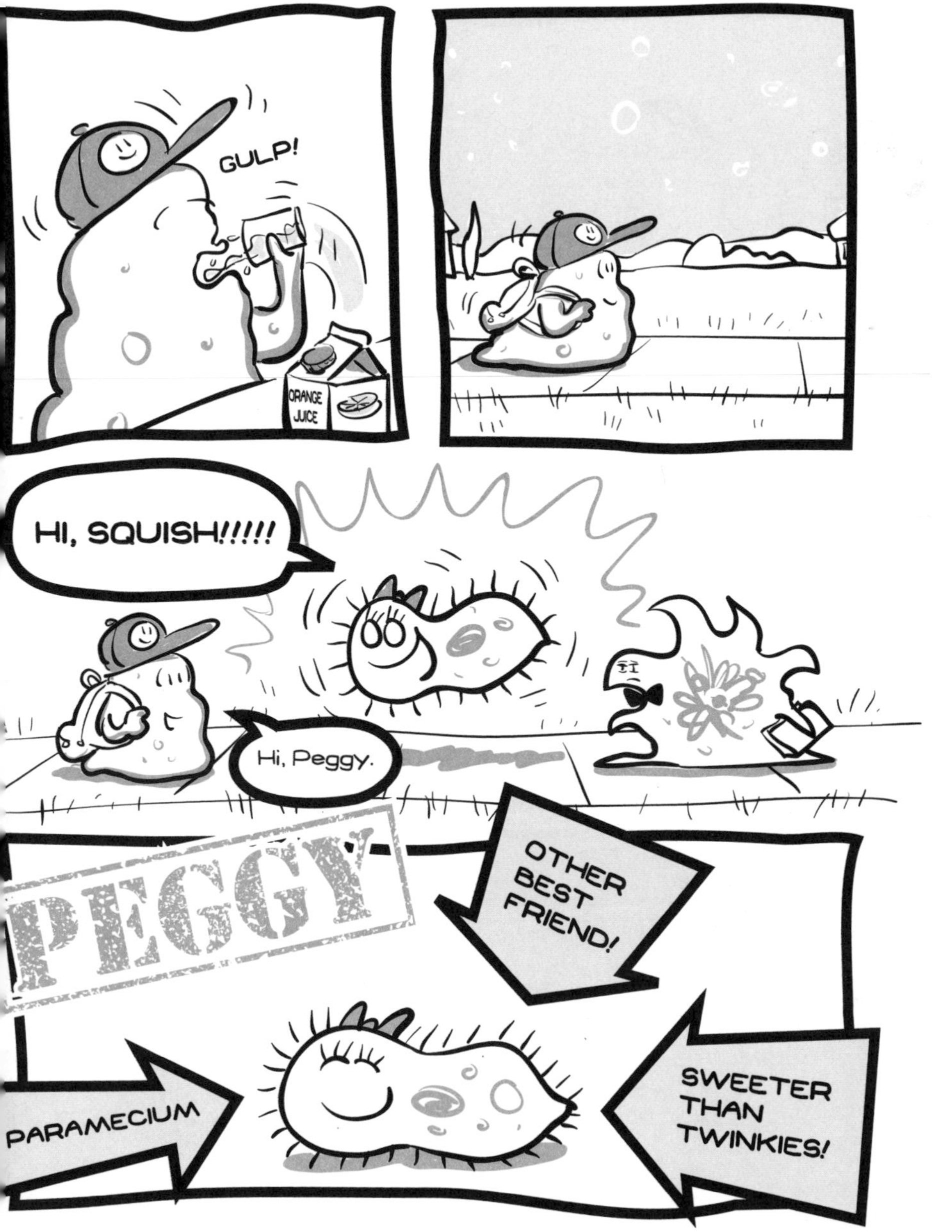
GULP!
ORANGE JUICE
HI, SQUISH!!!!!
Hi, Peggy.
PEGGY
OTHER BEST FRIEND!
PARAMECIUM
SWEETER THAN TWINKIES!

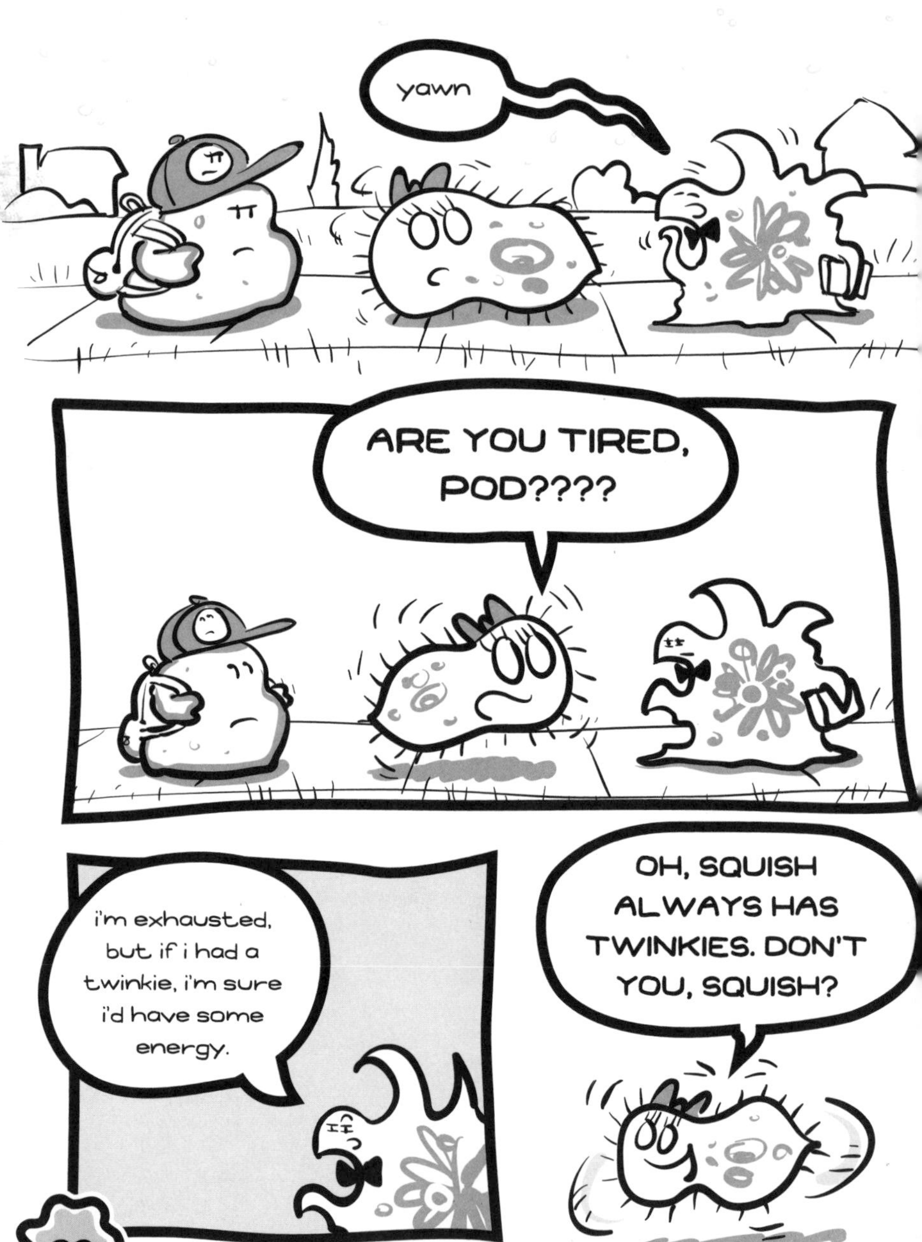
yawn
ARE YOU TIRED, POD????
i'm exhausted, but if i had a twinkie, i'm sure i'd have some energy.
OH, SQUISH ALWAYS HAS TWINKIES. DON'T YOU, SQUISH?

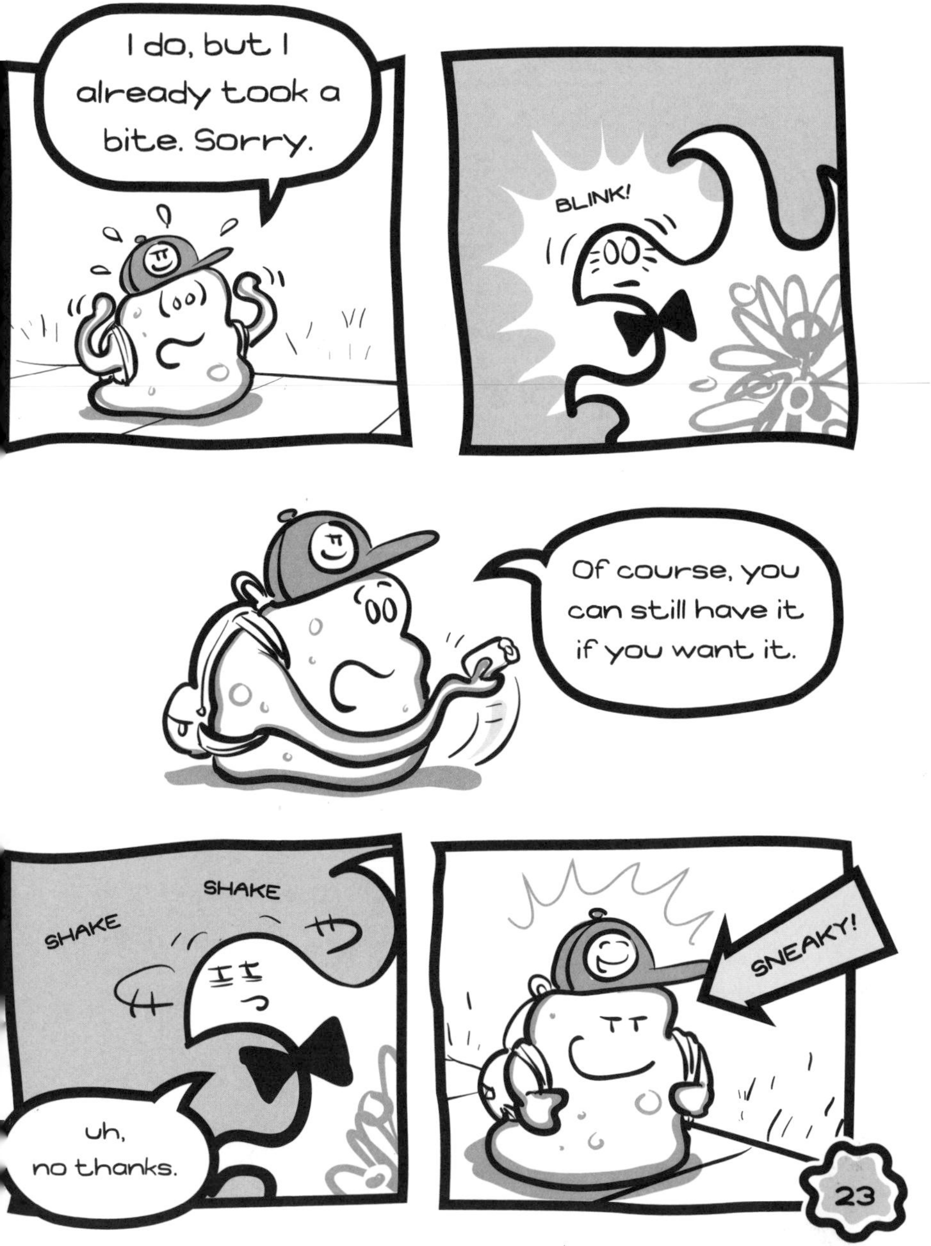
I do, but I already took a bite. Sorry.
BLINK!
Of course, you can still have it if you want it.
SHAKE
SHAKE
uh, no thanks.
SNEAKY!

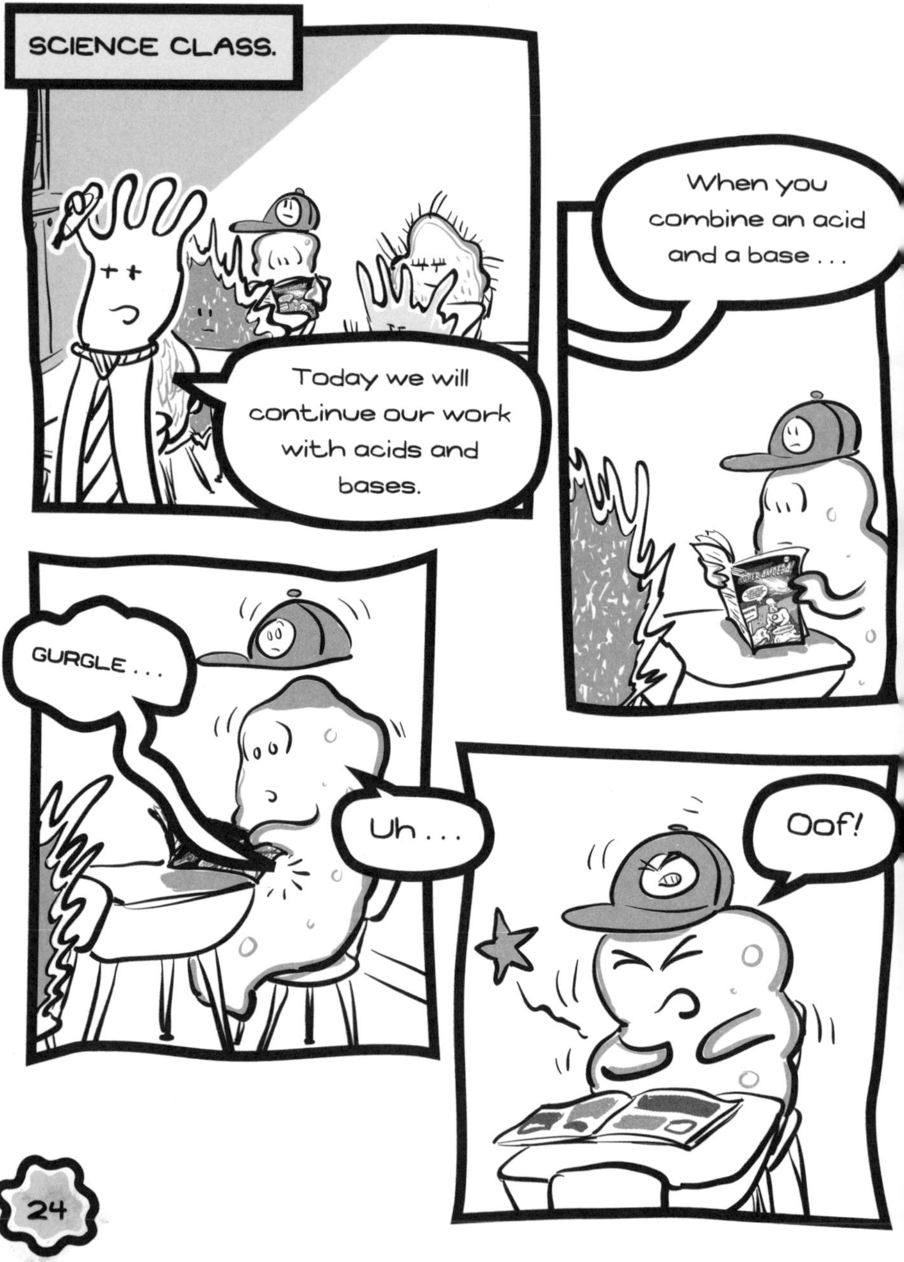
SCIENCE CLASS.
Today we will continue our work with acids and bases.
When you combine an acid and a base . . .
GURGLE . . .
Uh . . .
Oof!

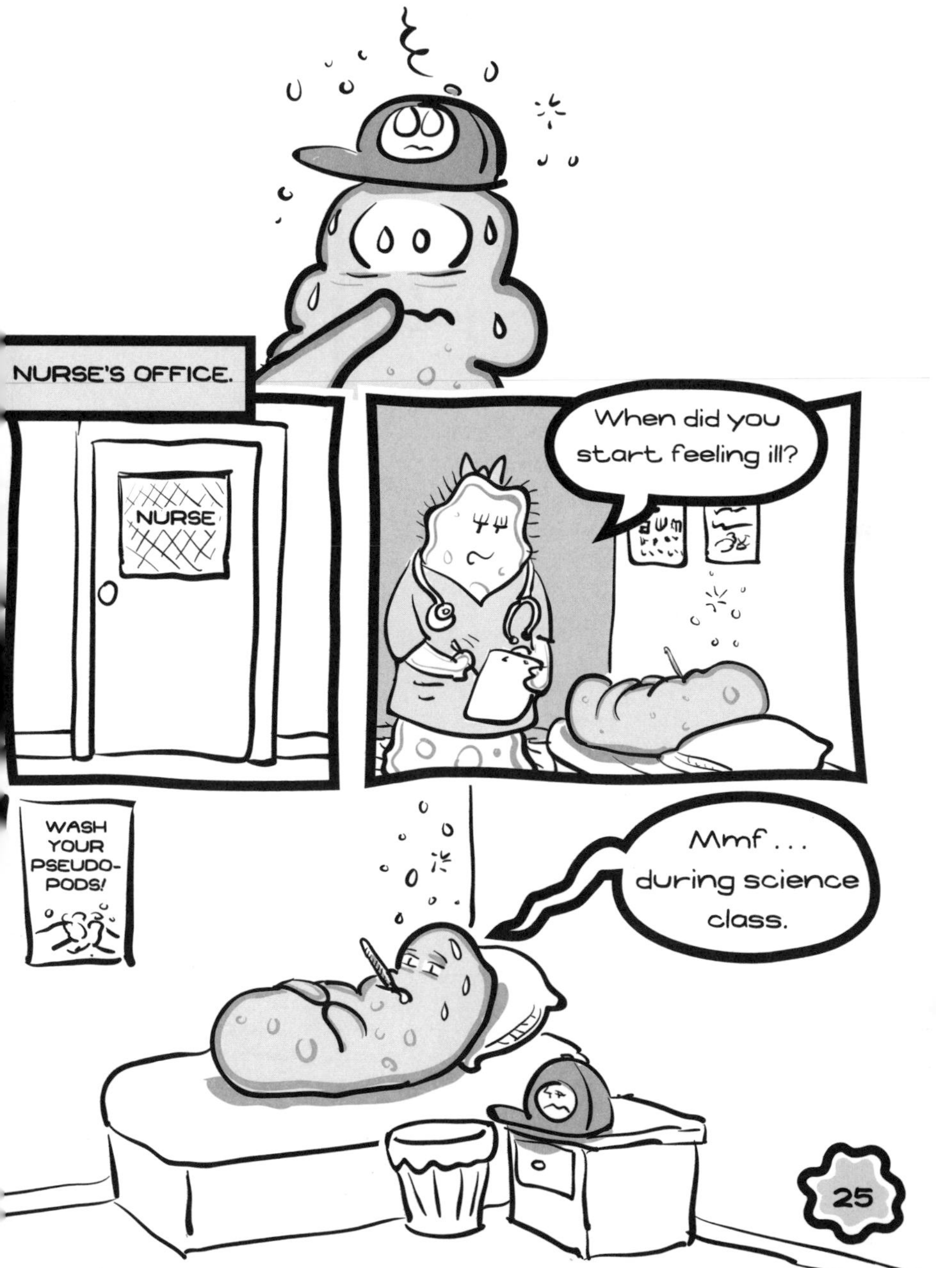
NURSE'S OFFICE.
NURSE
When did you start feeling ill?
WASH YOUR PSEUDO-PODS!
Mmf . . . during science class.

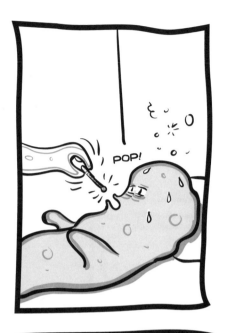

POP!

Well, you don't have a fever, so I think you should be able to go back to class and—

SHAKE SHAKE

BARF!

Then again, maybe I'll call your parents.

BARF!

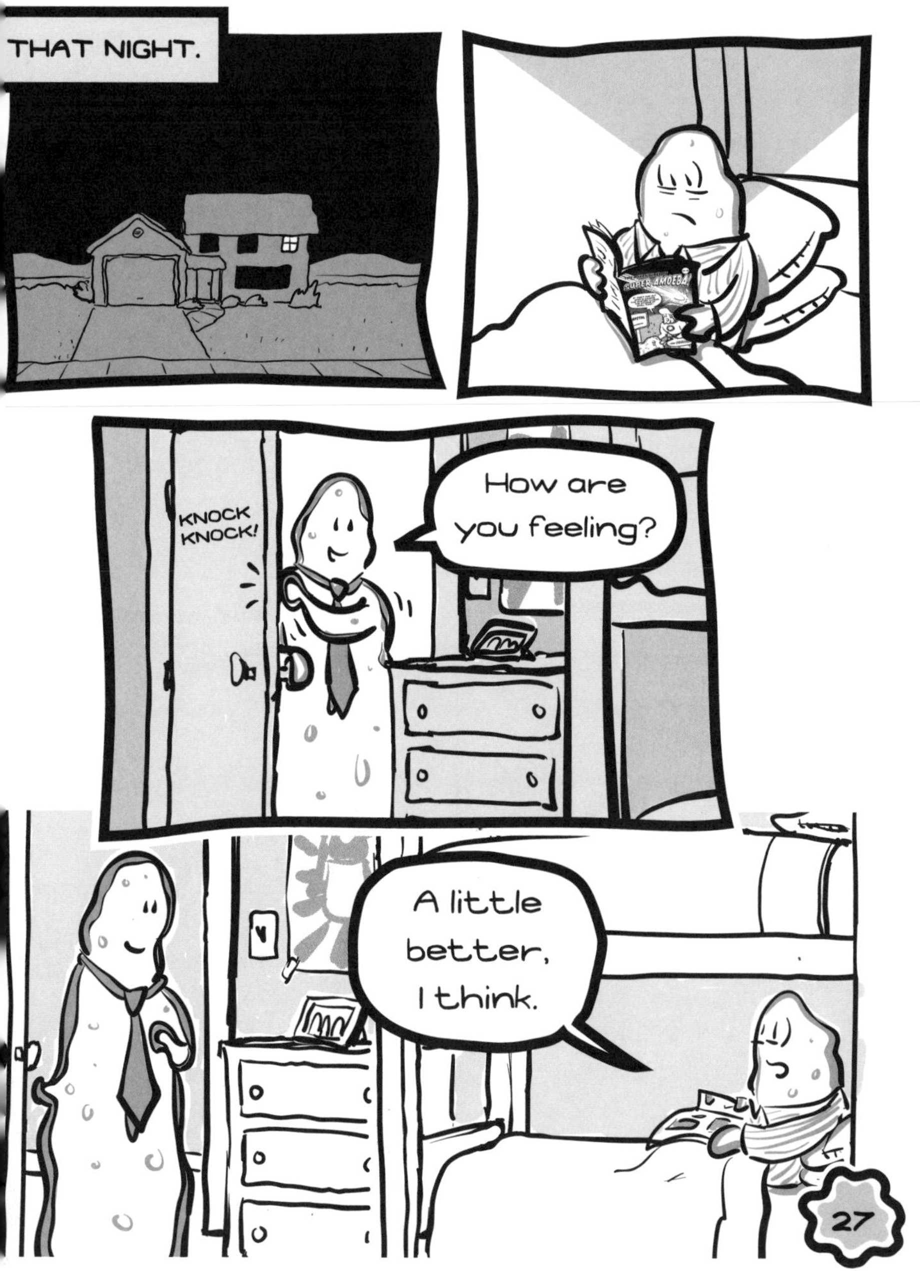
THAT NIGHT.
KNOCK KNOCK!
How are you feeling?
A little better, I think.

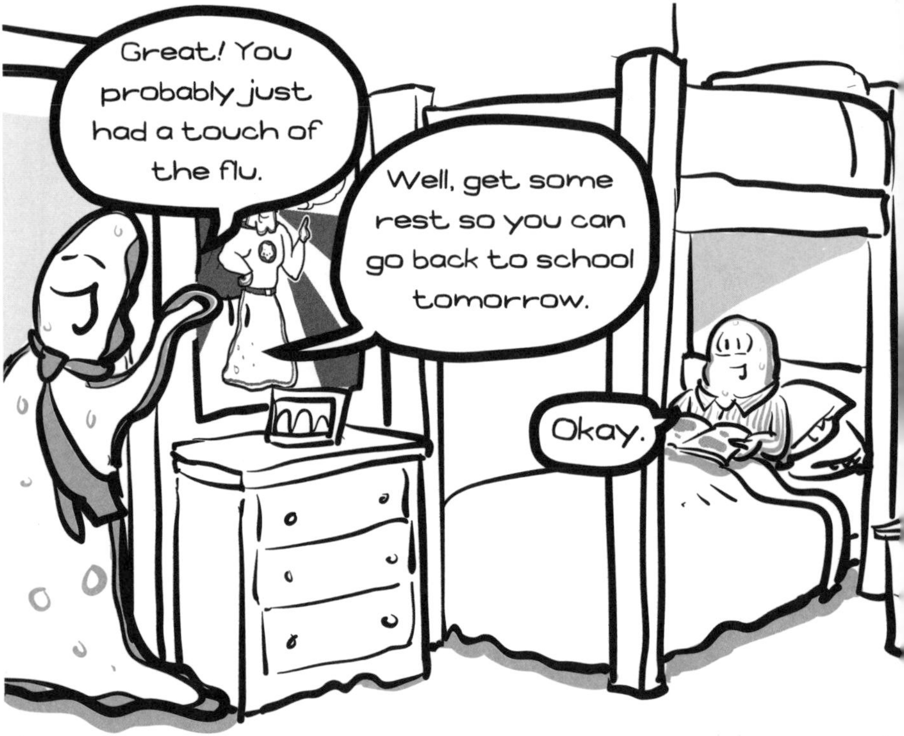
Great! You probably just had a touch of the flu.
Well, get some rest so you can go back to school tomorrow.
Okay.

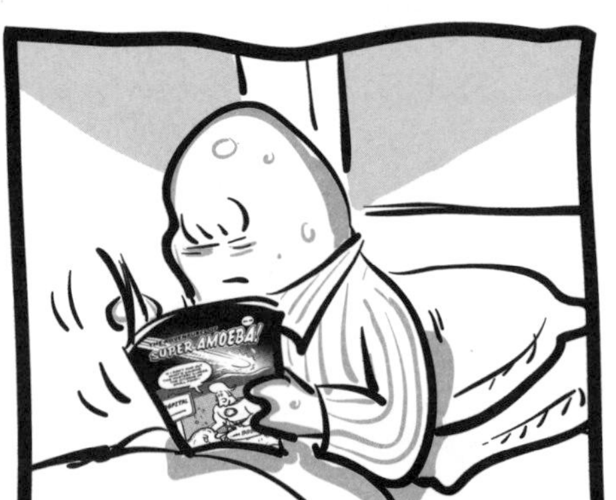
SUPER AMOEBA!

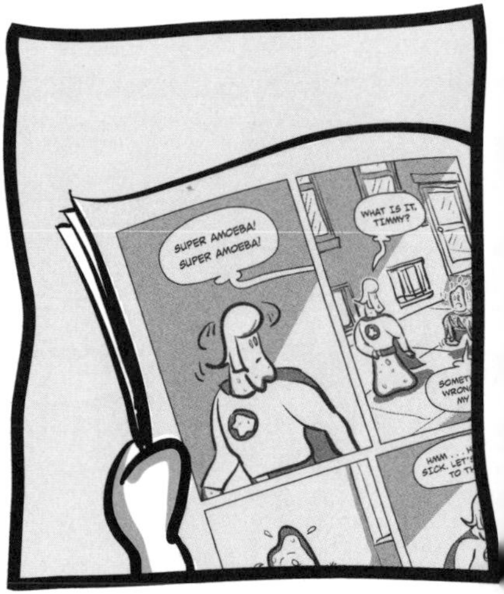
SUPER AMOEBA! SUPER AMOEBA!
WHAT IS IT, TIMMY?

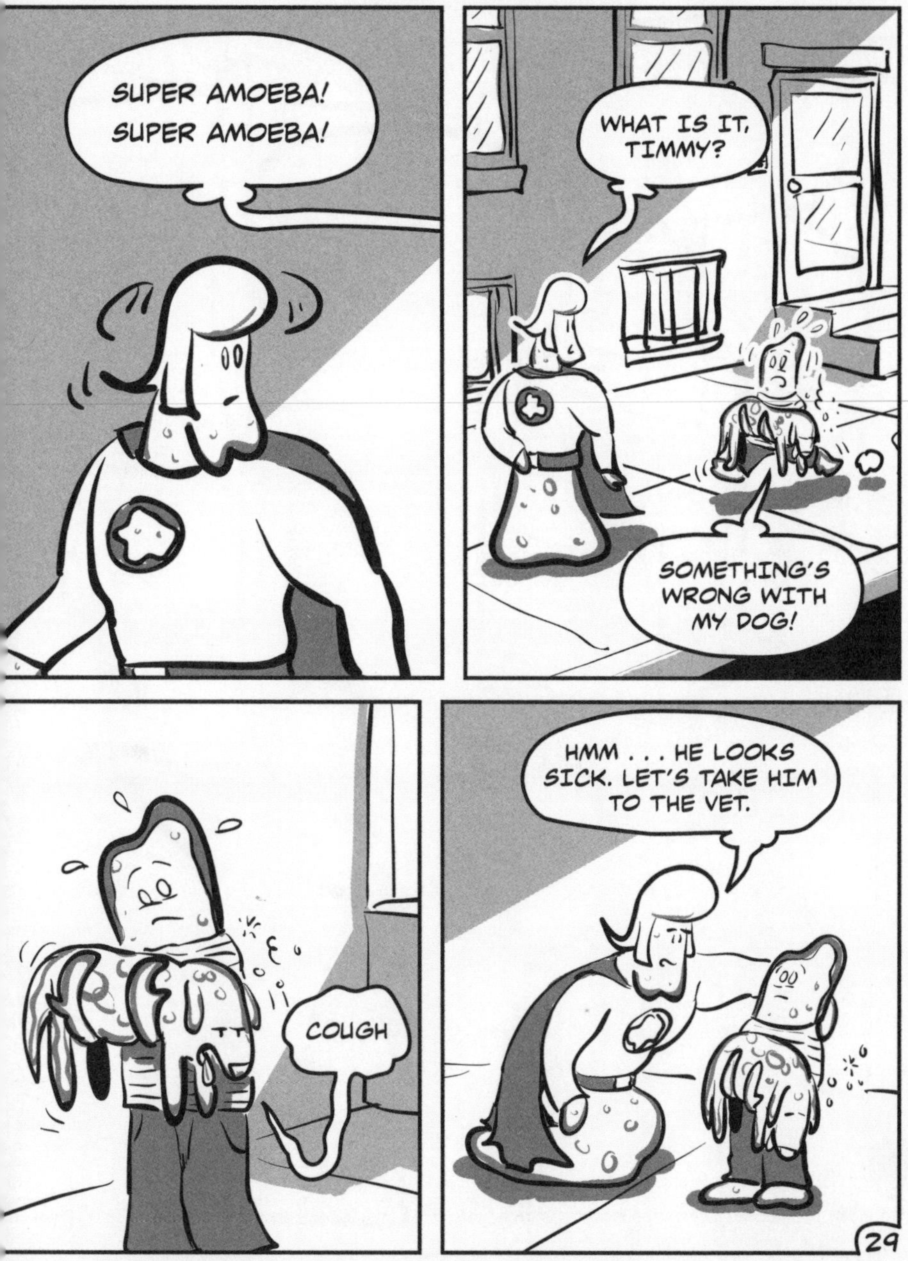
SUPER AMOEBA! SUPER AMOEBA!
WHAT IS IT, TIMMY?
SOMETHING'S WRONG WITH MY DOG!
COUGH
HMM . . . HE LOOKS SICK. LET'S TAKE HIM TO THE VET.

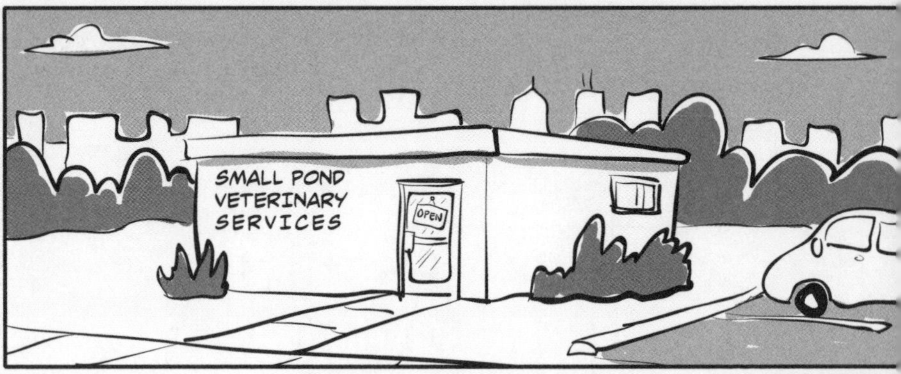
SMALL POND
VETERINARY
SERVICES
OPEN

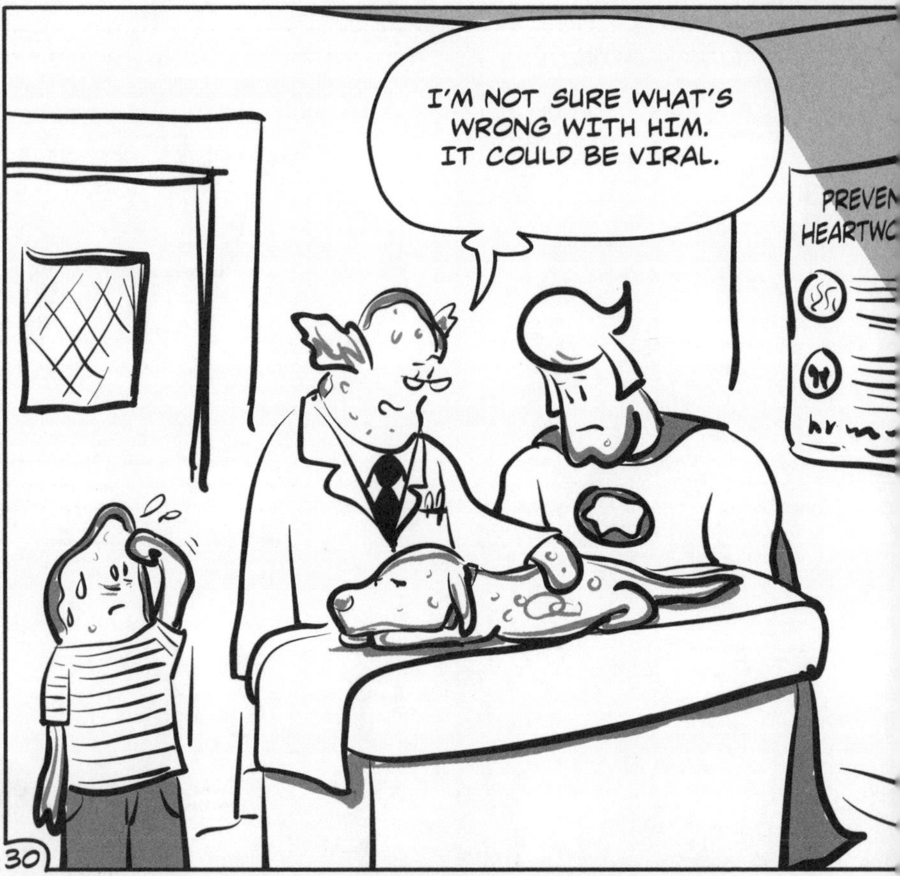
I'M NOT SURE WHAT'S WRONG WITH HIM. IT COULD BE VIRAL.
PREVEN
HEARTWO

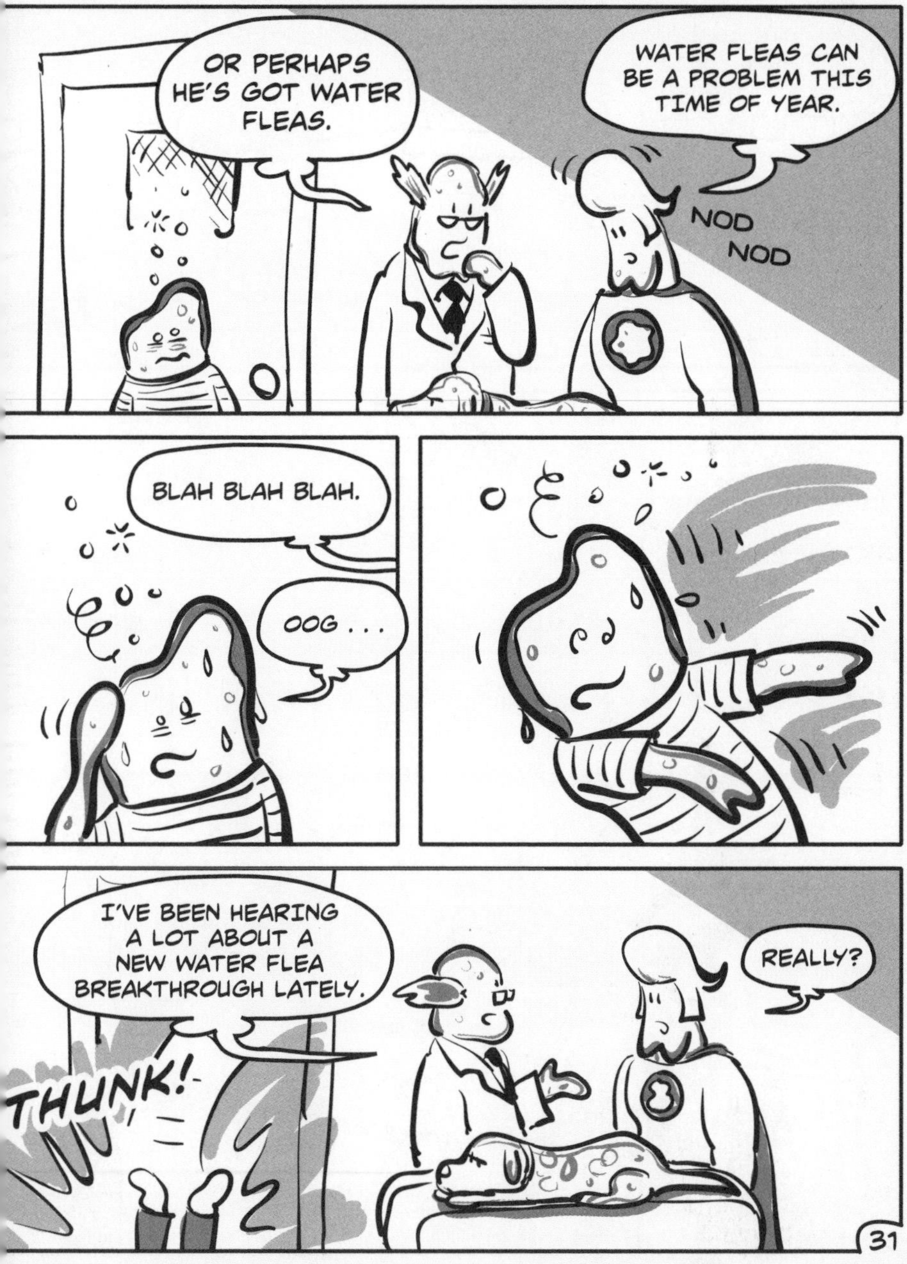
OR PERHAPS HE'S GOT WATER FLEAS.
WATER FLEAS CAN BE A PROBLEM THIS TIME OF YEAR.
NOD NOD
BLAH BLAH BLAH.
OOG . . .
I'VE BEEN HEARING A LOT ABOUT A NEW WATER FLEA BREAKTHROUGH LATELY.
REALLY?
THUNK!

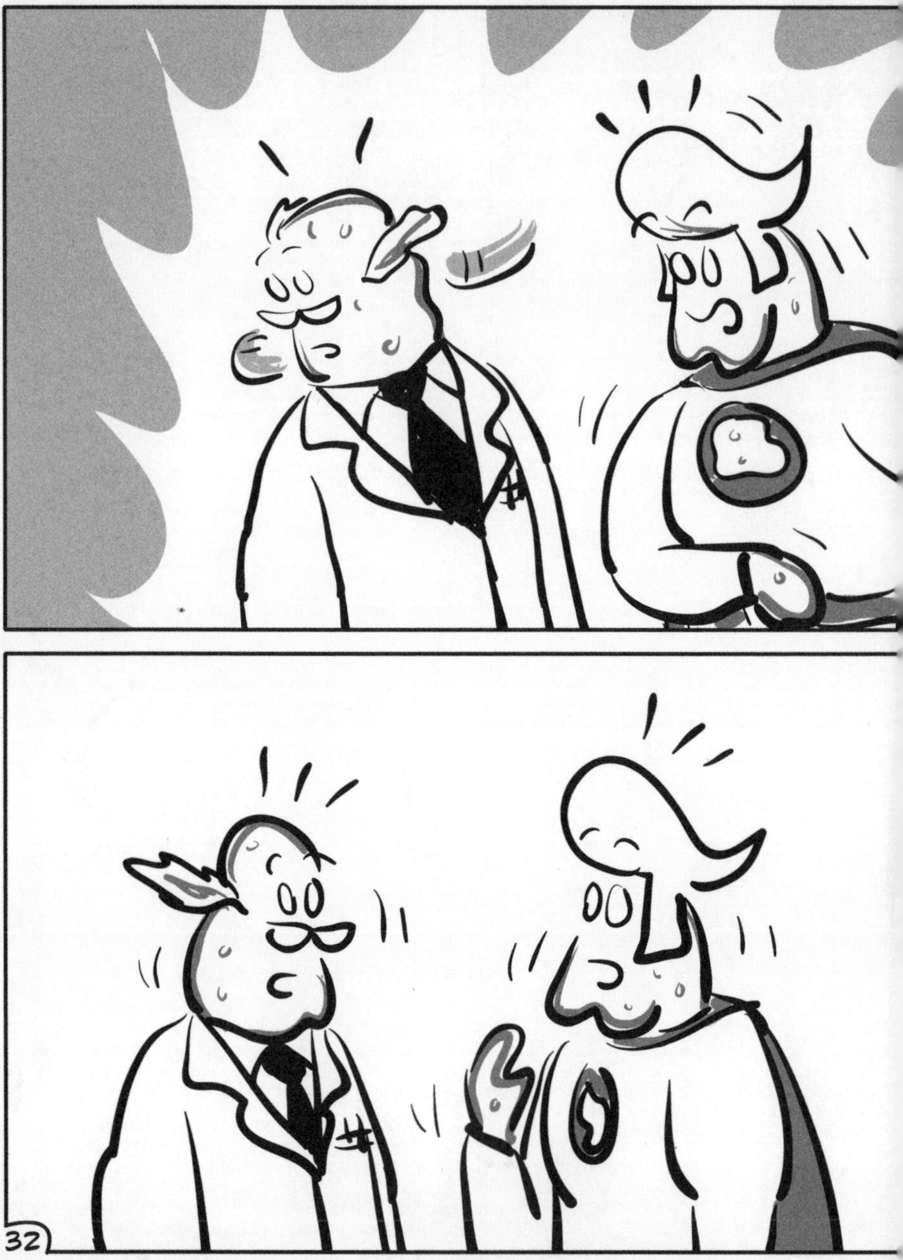

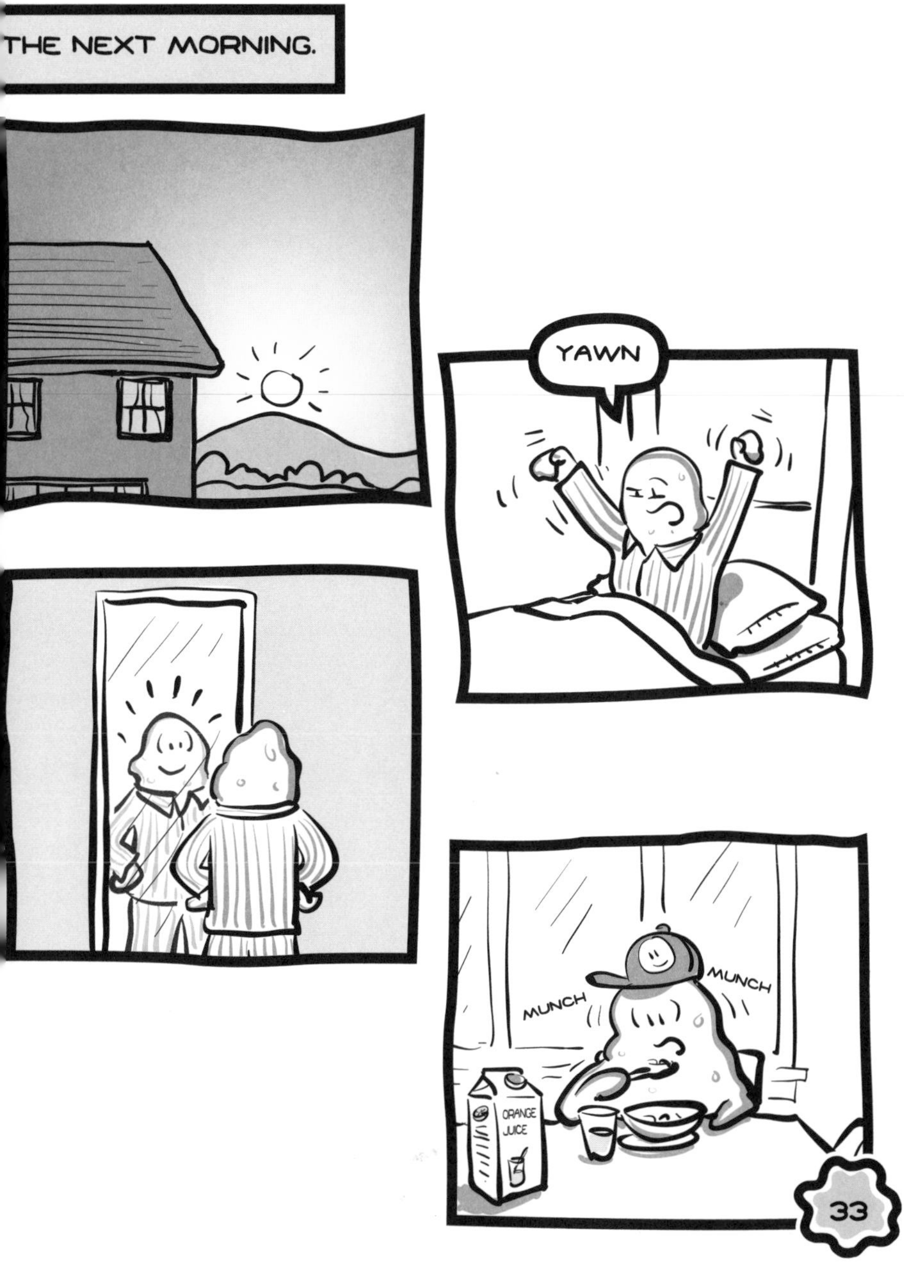
THE NEXT MORNING.
YAWN
MUNCH
MUNCH
ORANGE JUICE

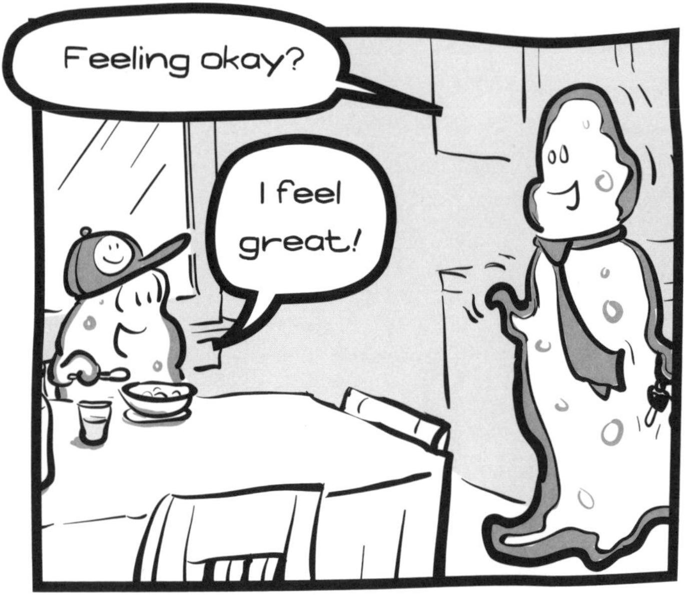

Feeling okay?
I feel great!

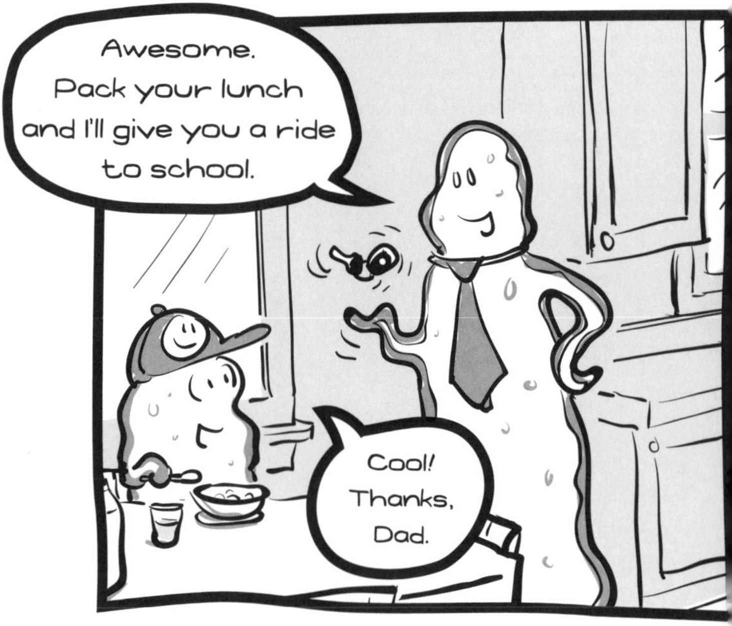

Awesome. Pack your lunch and I'll give you a ride to school.
Cool! Thanks, Dad.

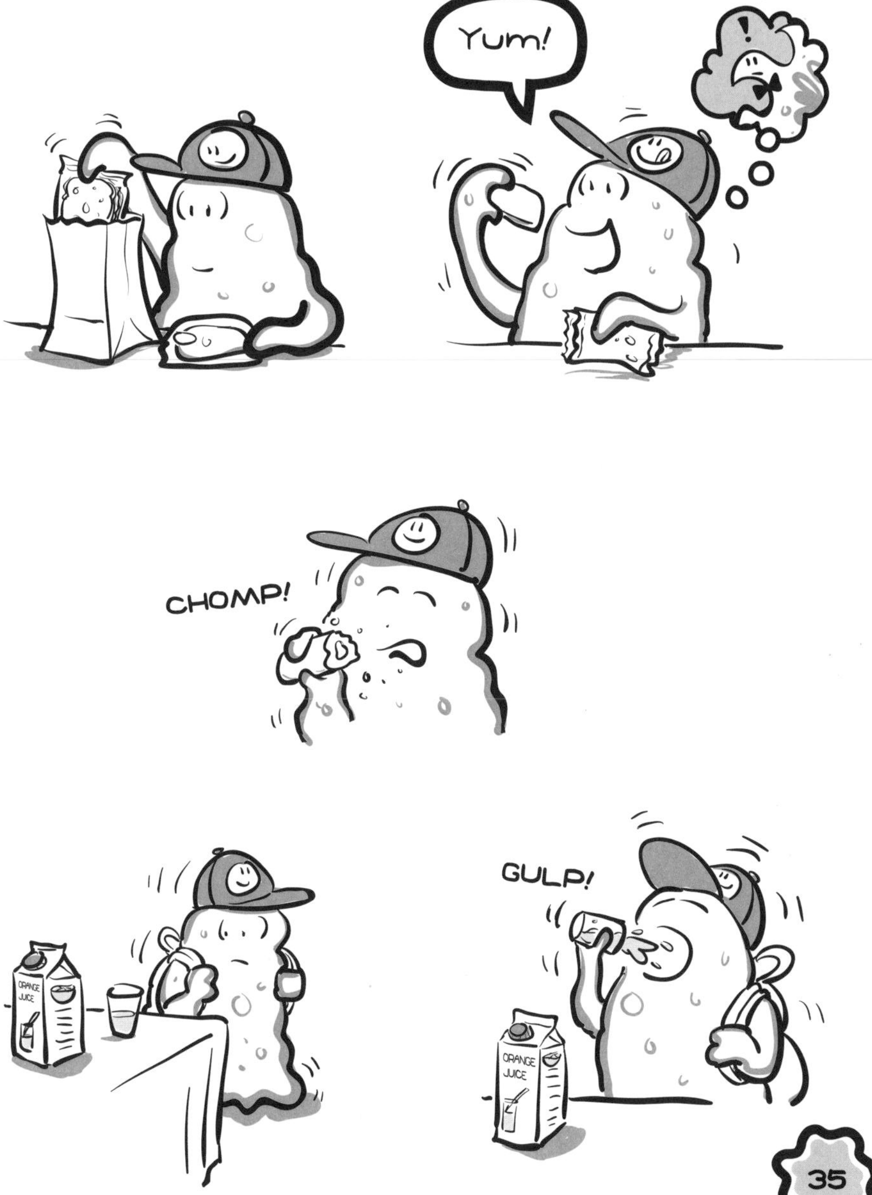
Yum!
!
CHOMP!
ORANGE JUICE
GULP!
ORANGE JUICE

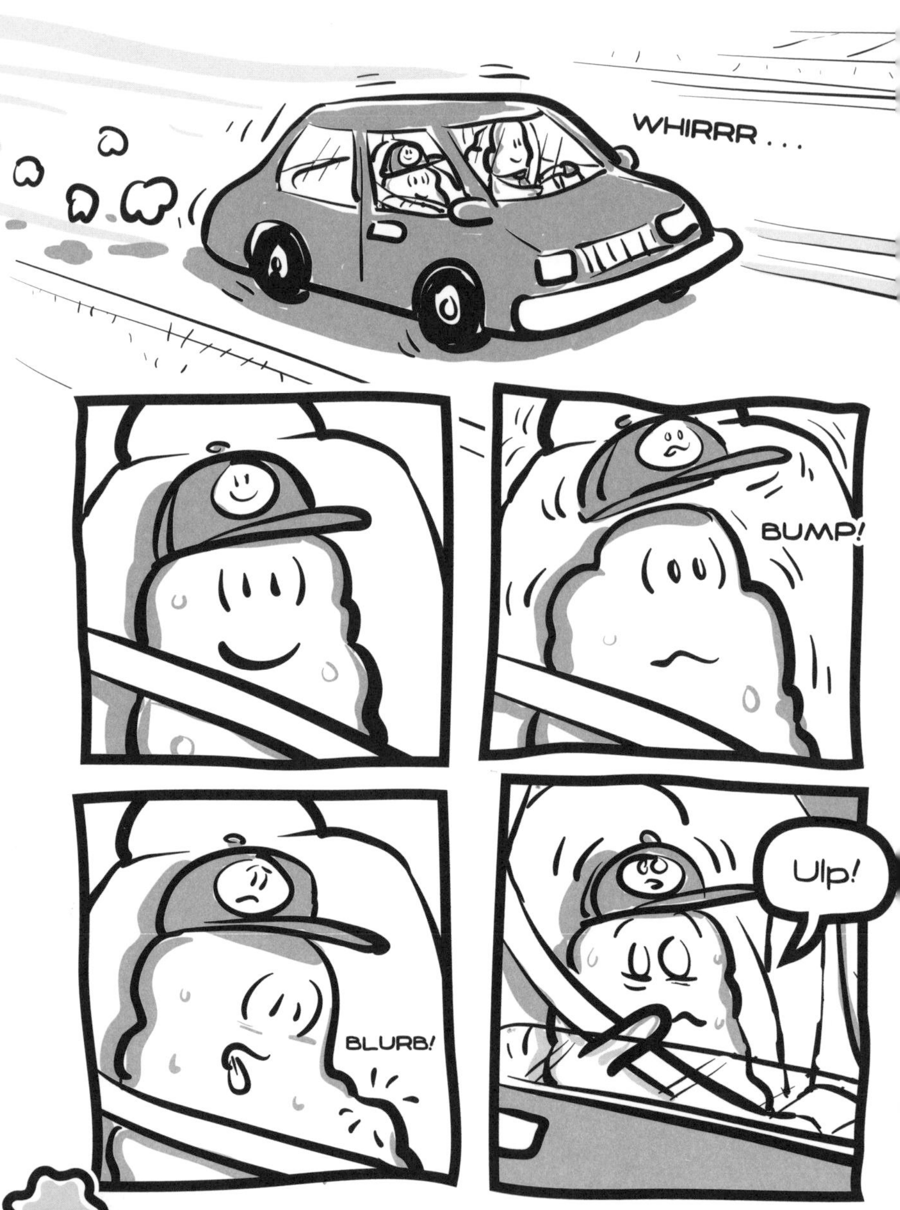
WHIRRR . . .
BUMP!
BLURB!
Ulp!

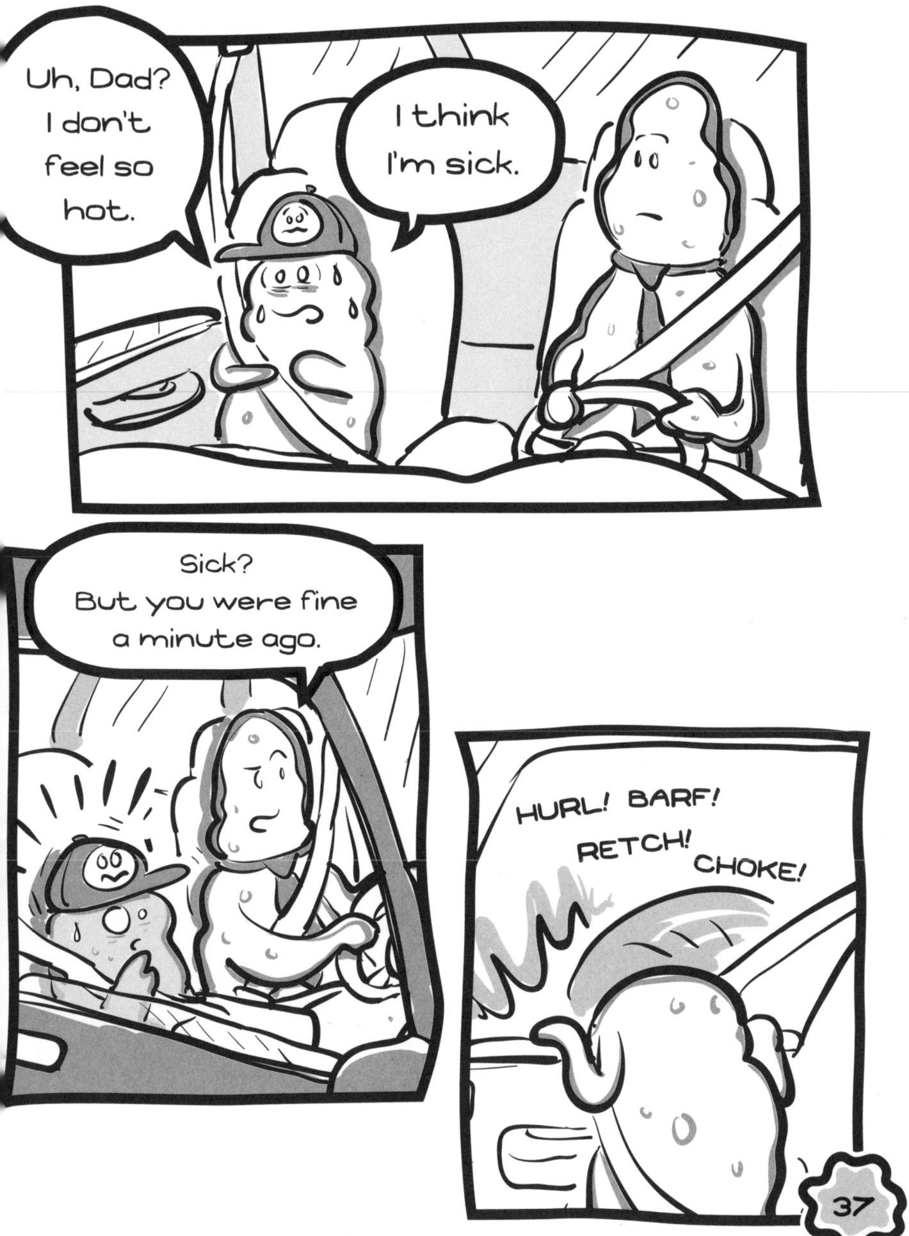
Uh, Dad? I don't feel so hot.
I think I'm sick.
Sick? But you were fine a minute ago.
HURL! BARF!
RETCH!
CHOKE!

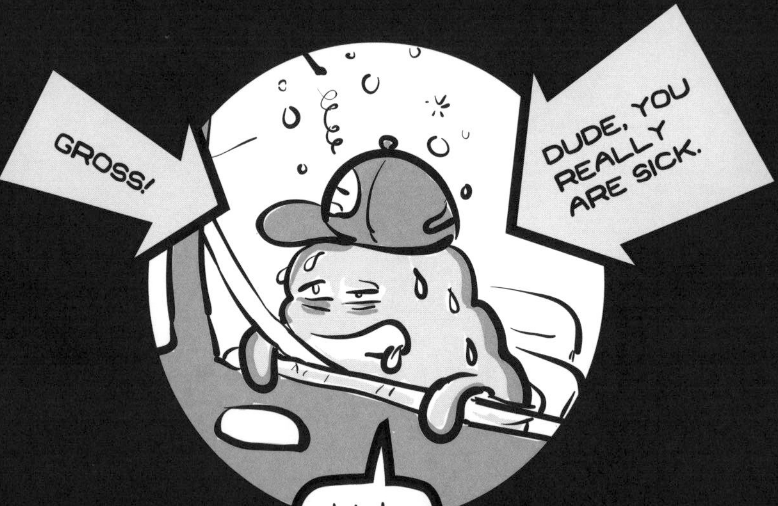
GROSS!
DUDE, YOU REALLY ARE SICK.
Ugh.

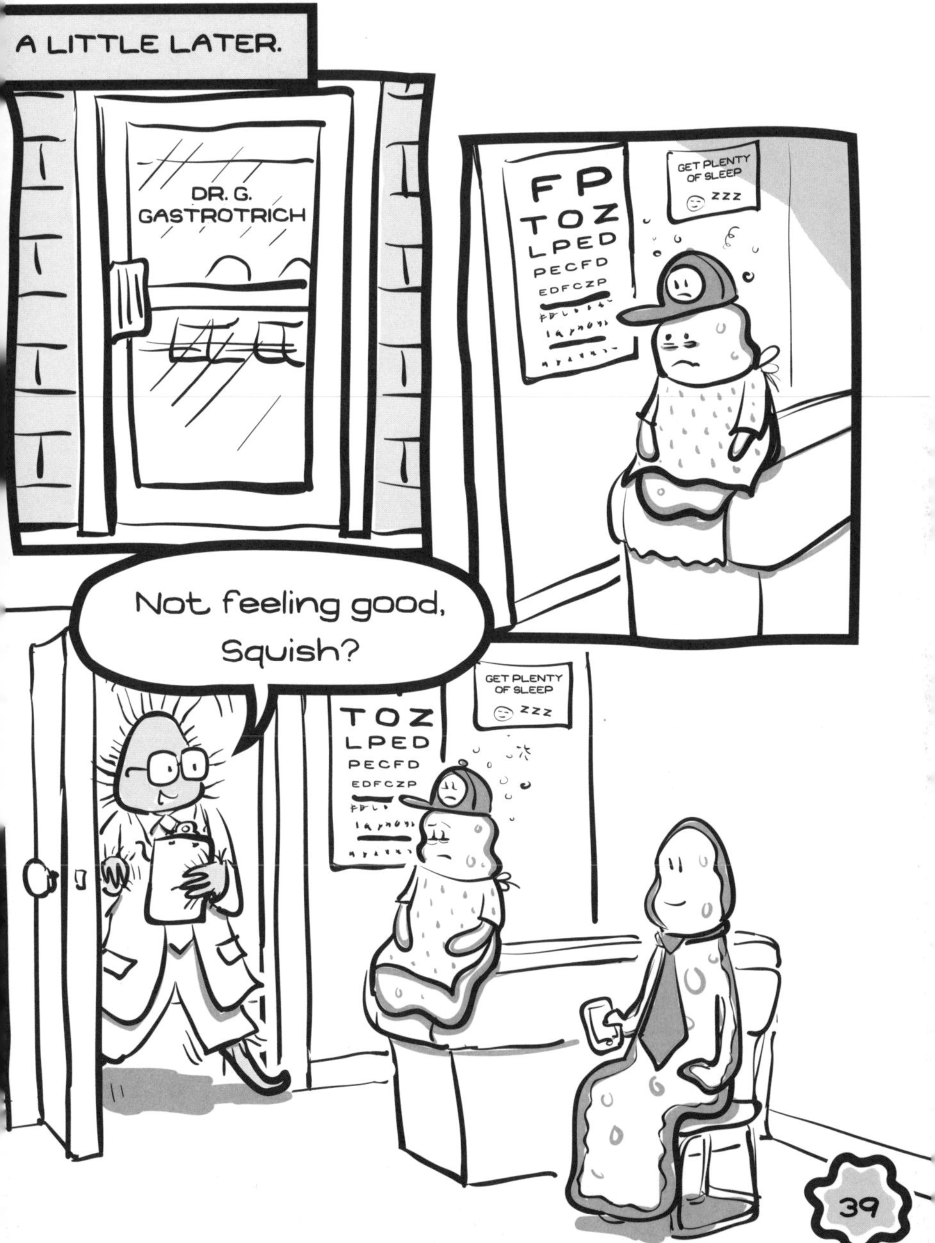
A LITTLE LATER.
DR. G. GASTROTRICH
F P
T O Z
L P E D
P E C F D
E D F C Z P
GET PLENTY OF SLEEP
ZZZ
Not feeling good, Squish?
T O Z
L P E D
P E C F D
E D F C Z P
GET PLENTY OF SLEEP
ZZZ

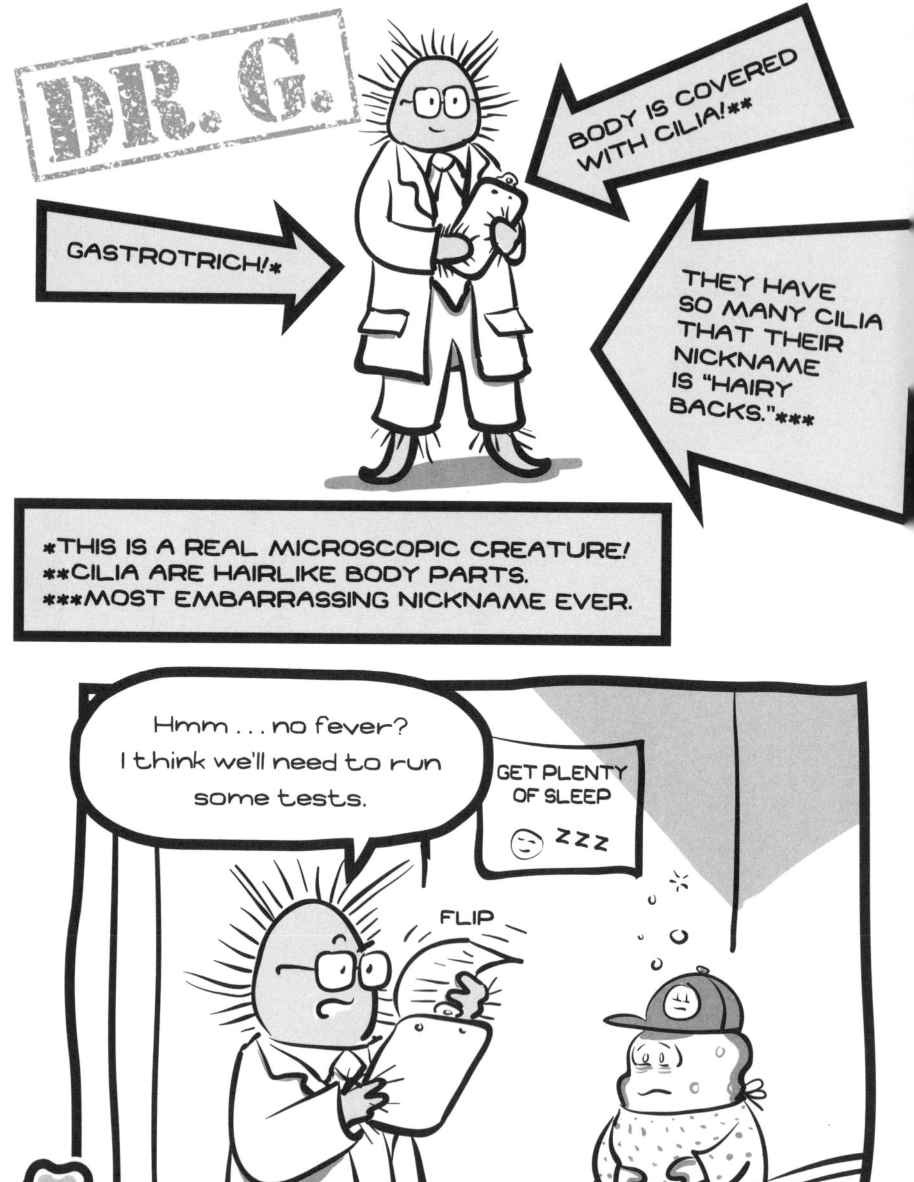
DR. G.
GASTROTRICH!*
BODY IS COVERED WITH CILIA!**
THEY HAVE SO MANY CILIA THAT THEIR NICKNAME IS "HAIRY BACKS."***
*THIS IS A REAL MICROSCOPIC CREATURE!
**CILIA ARE HAIRLIKE BODY PARTS.
***MOST EMBARRASSING NICKNAME EVER.
Hmm . . . no fever? I think we'll need to run some tests.
GET PLENTY OF SLEEP
ZZZ
FLIP

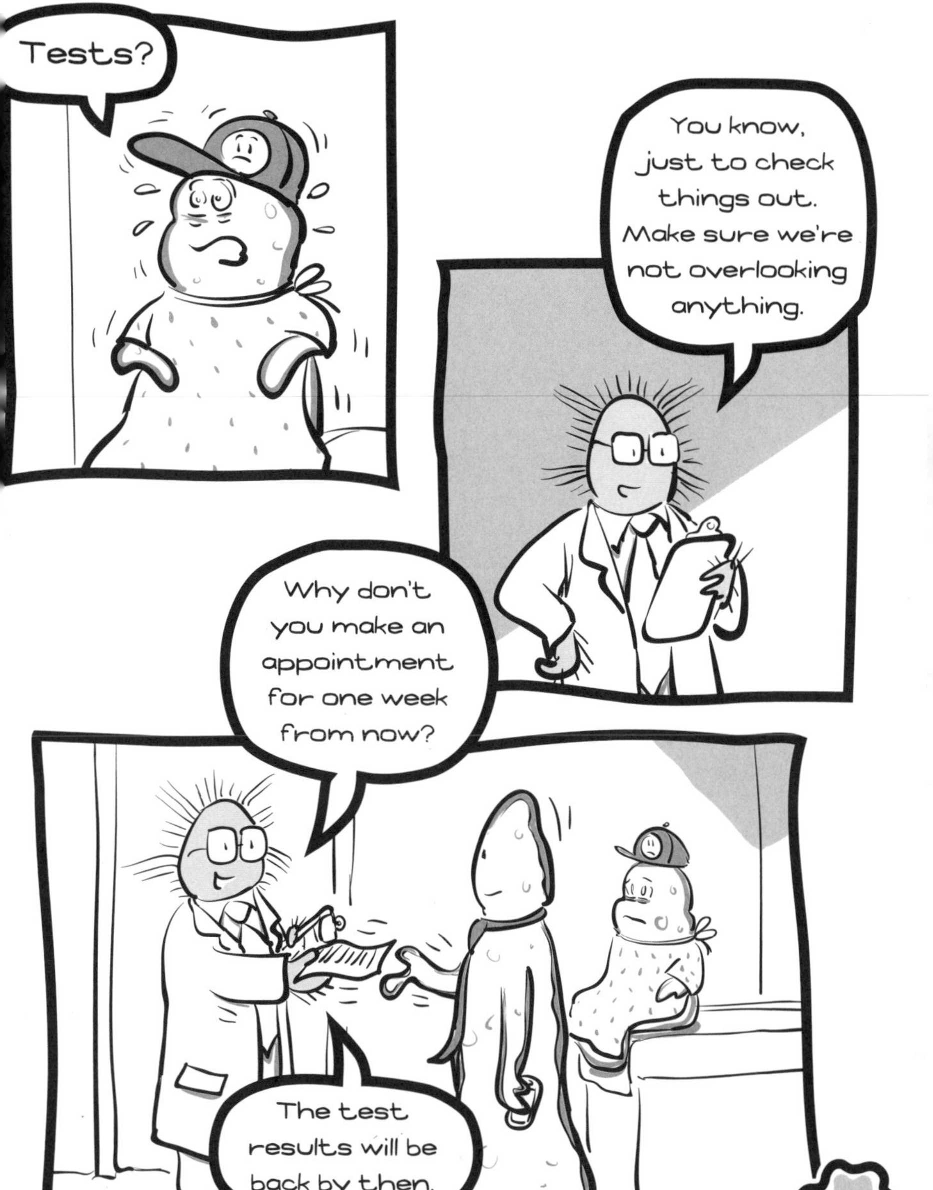
Tests?
You know, just to check things out. Make sure we're not overlooking anything.
Why don't you make an appointment for one week from now?
The test results will be back by then.

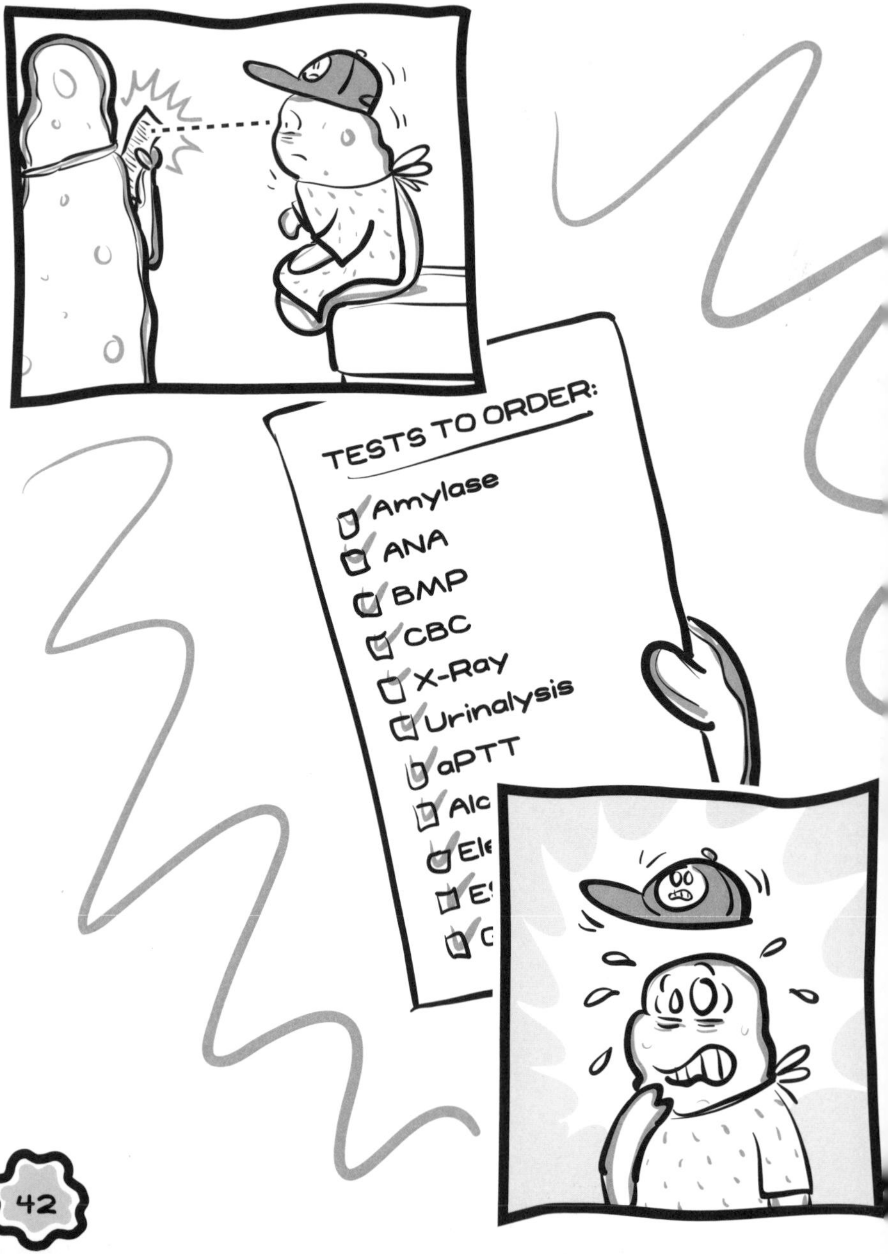
TESTS TO ORDER:
Amylase
ANA
BMP
CBC
X-Ray
Urinalysis
aPTT

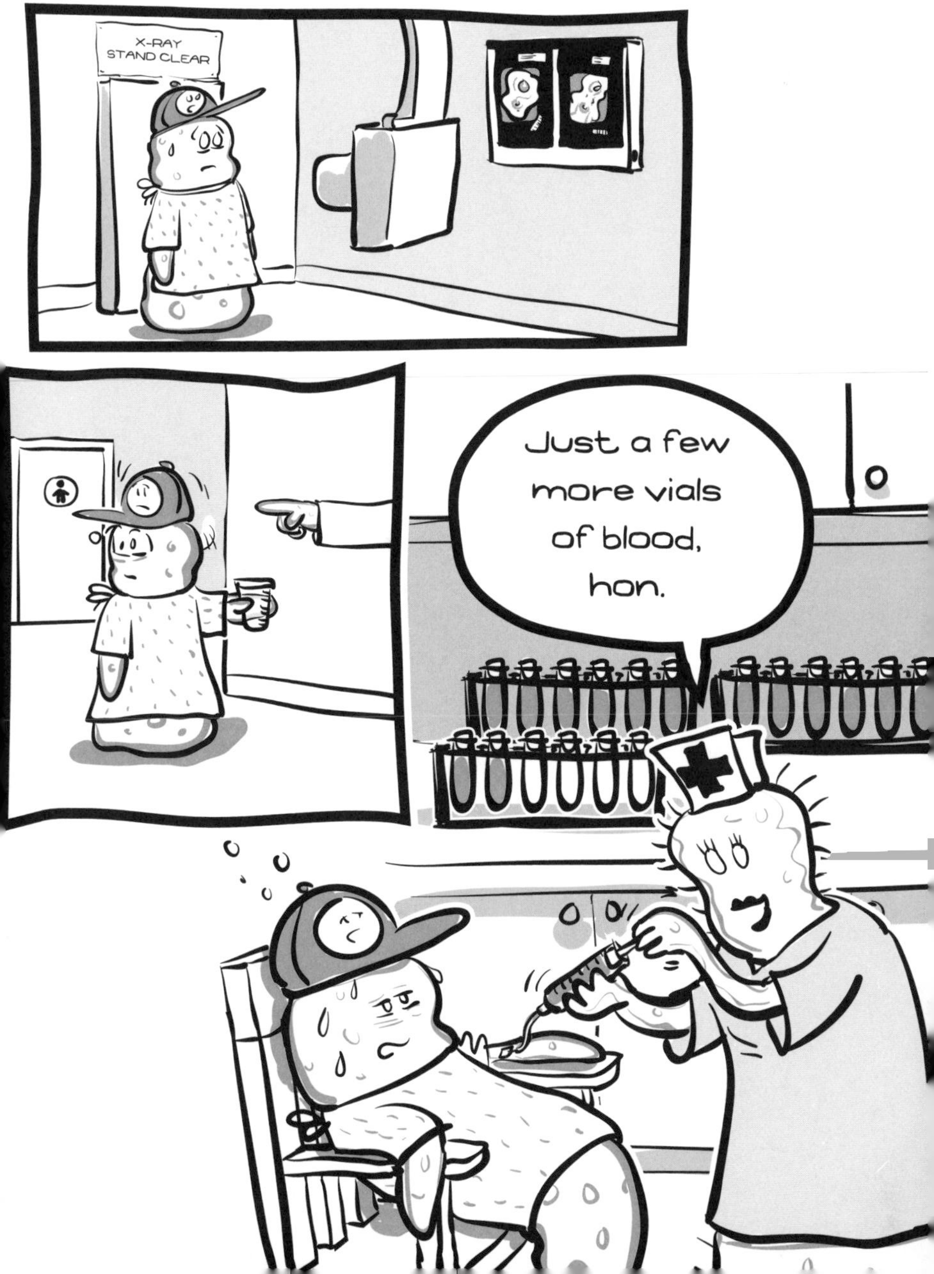
X-RAY
STAND CLEAR
Just a few more vials of blood, hon.

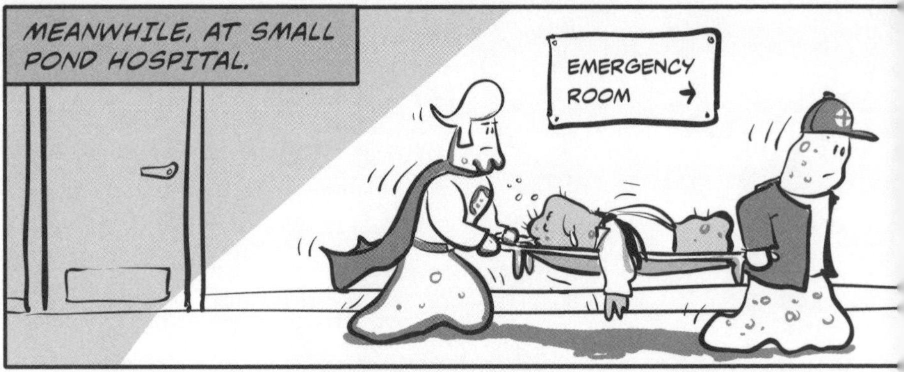
MEANWHILE, AT SMALL POND HOSPITAL.
EMERGENCY ROOM →

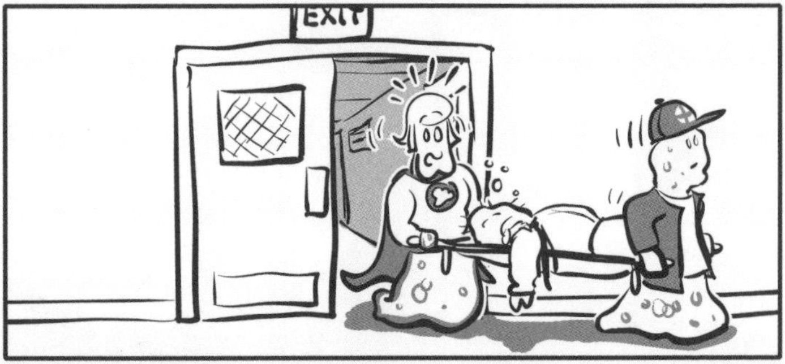
EXIT

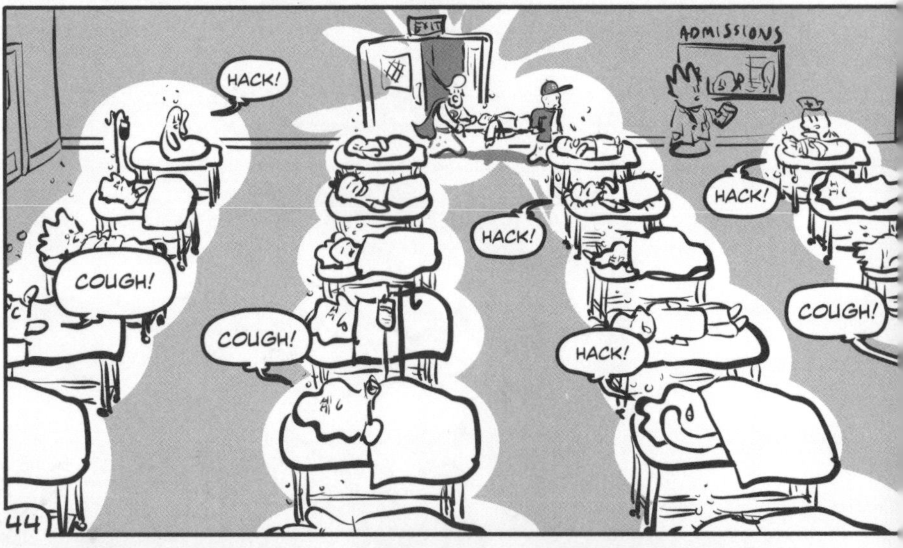
EXIT
ADMISSIONS
HACK!
HACK!
HACK!
COUGH!
COUGH!
HACK!
COUGH!

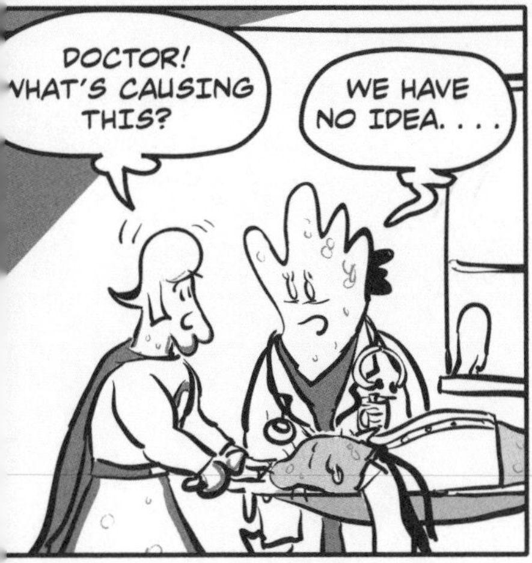
DOCTOR! WHAT'S CAUSING THIS?
WE HAVE NO IDEA. . . .

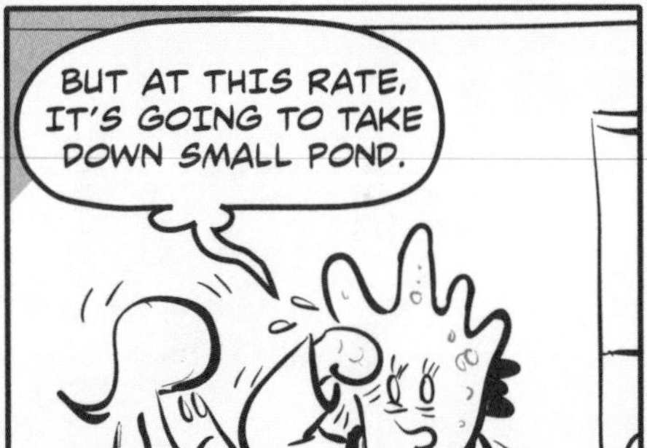
BUT AT THIS RATE, IT'S GOING TO TAKE DOWN SMALL POND.

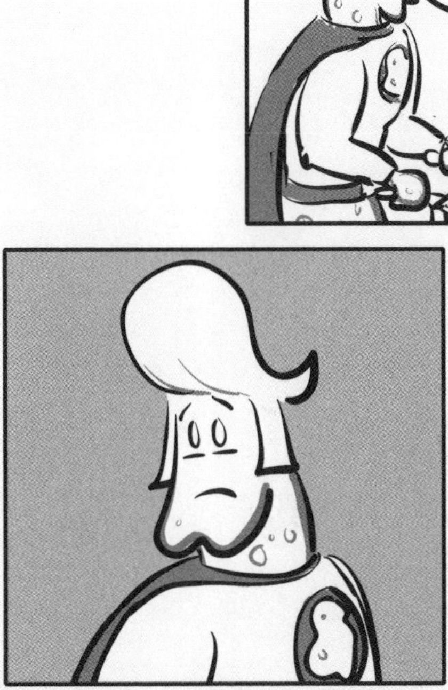

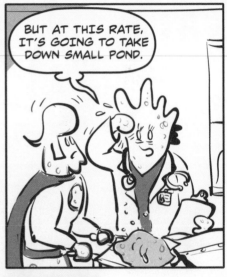

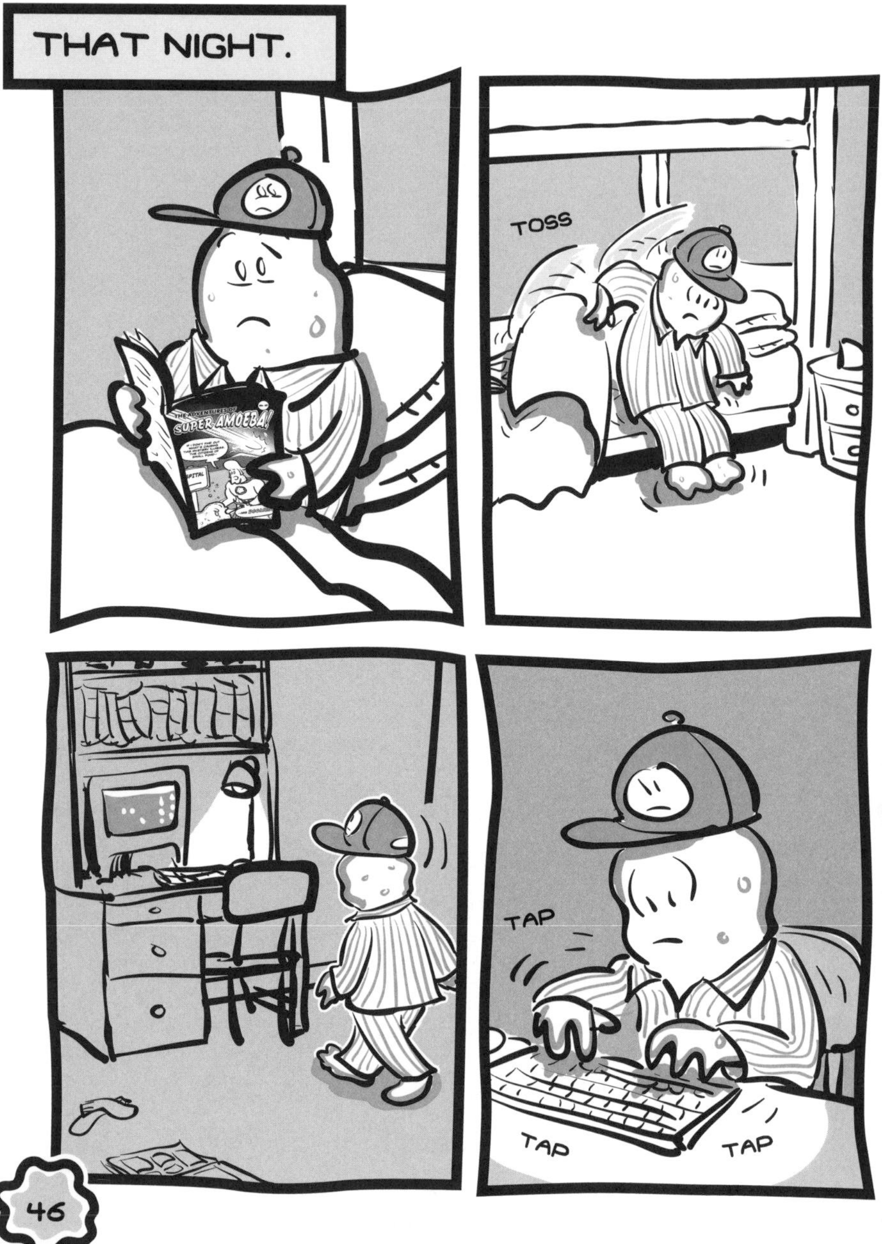
THAT NIGHT.
THE ADVENTURES OF
SUPER AMOEBA!
TOSS
TAP
TAP
TAP

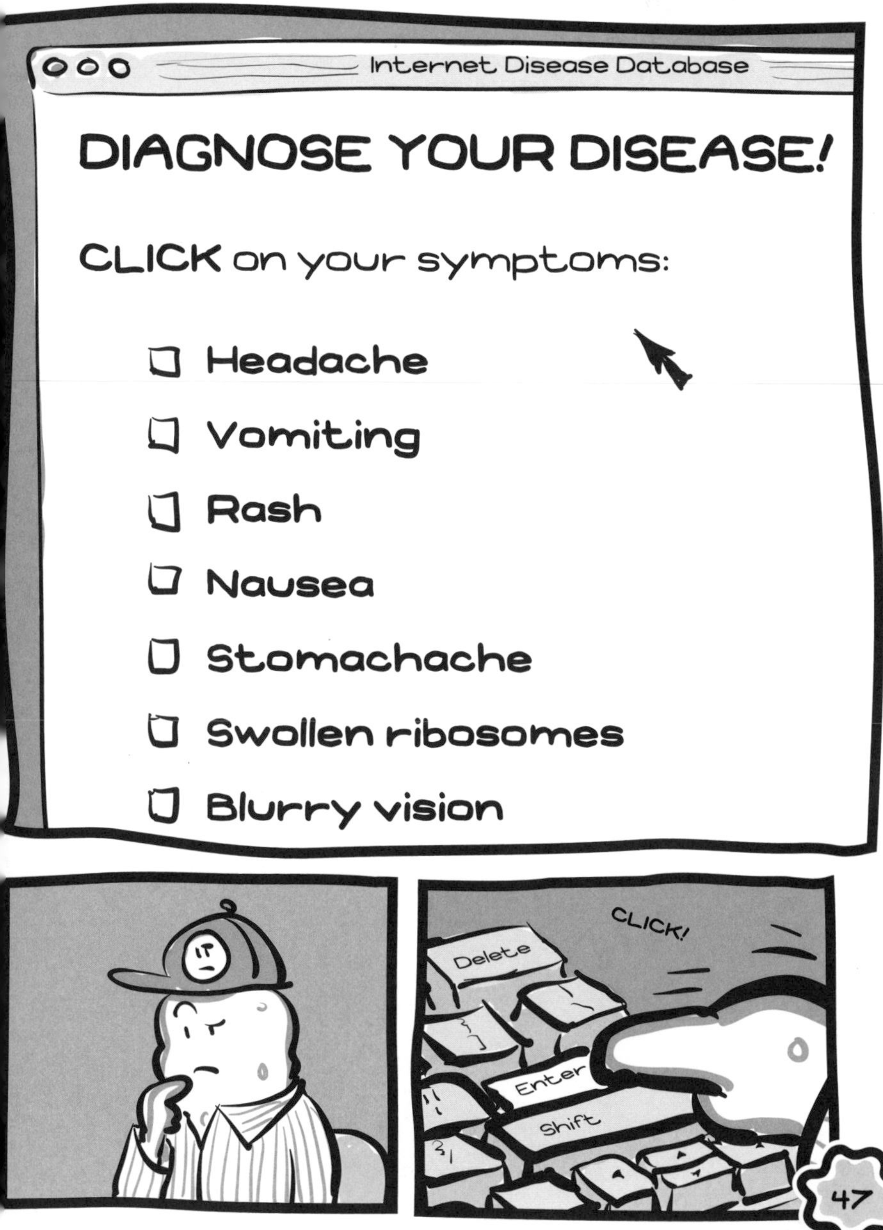

Internet Disease Database
DIAGNOSE YOUR DISEASE!
CLICK on your symptoms:
Headache
Vomiting
Rash
Nausea
Stomachache
Swollen ribosomes
Blurry vision
CLICK!
Delete
Enter
Shift

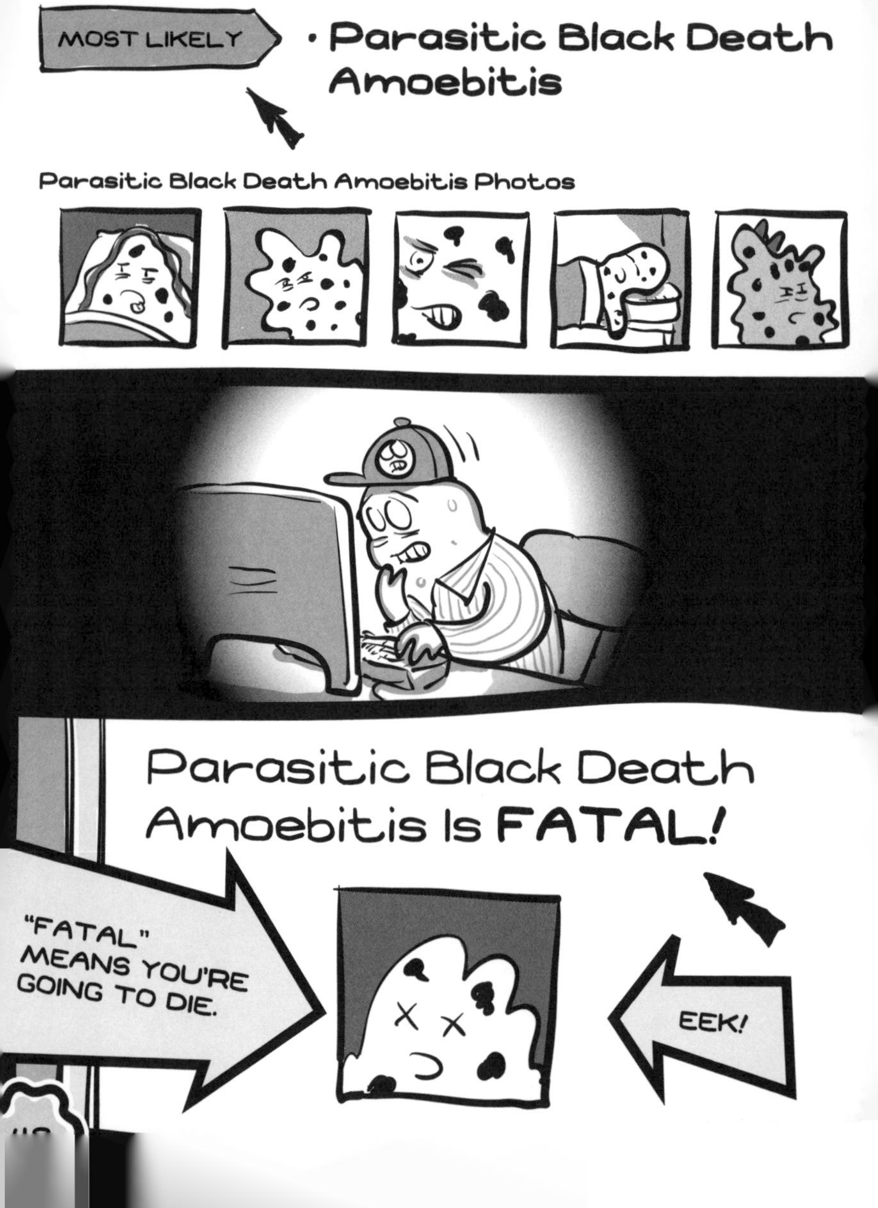
MOST LIKELY
• Parasitic Black Death Amoebitis
Parasitic Black Death Amoebitis Photos
Parasitic Black Death Amoebitis Is FATAL!
"FATAL" MEANS YOU'RE GOING TO DIE.
EEK!

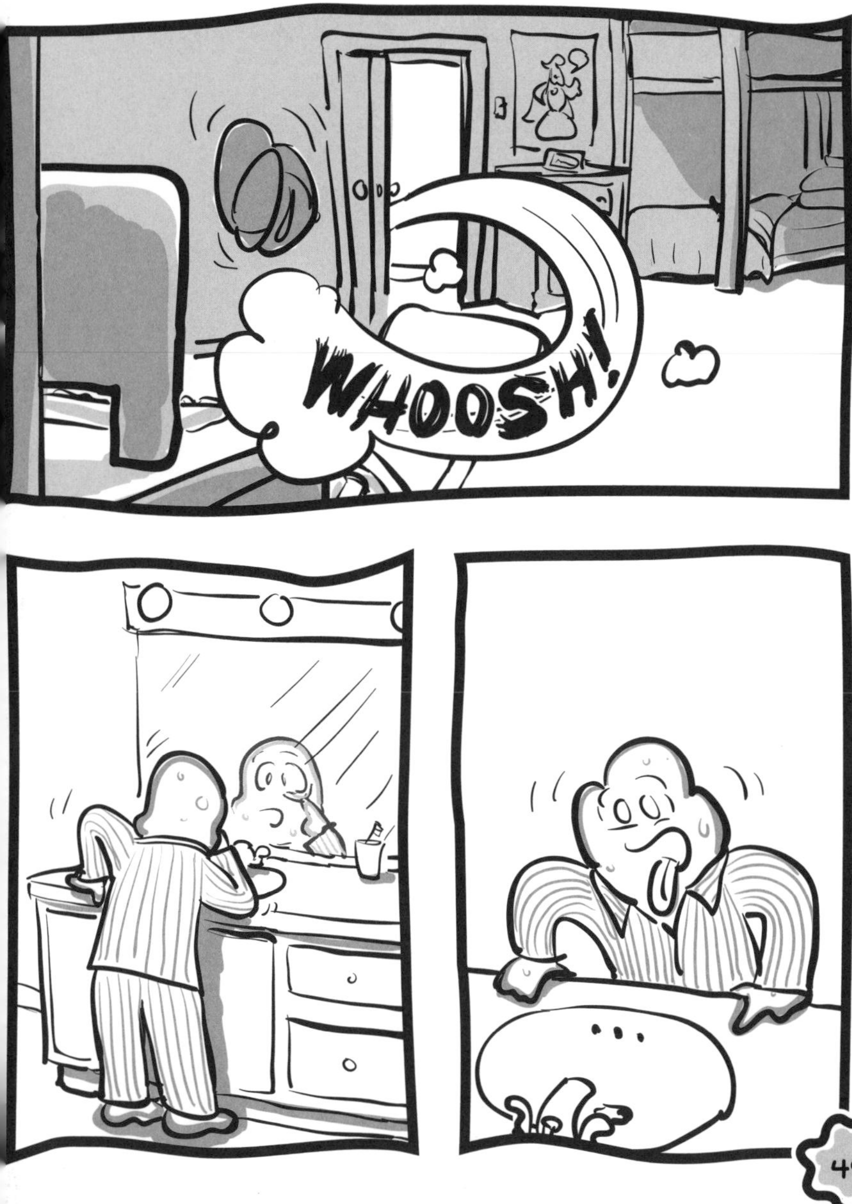
WHOOSH!

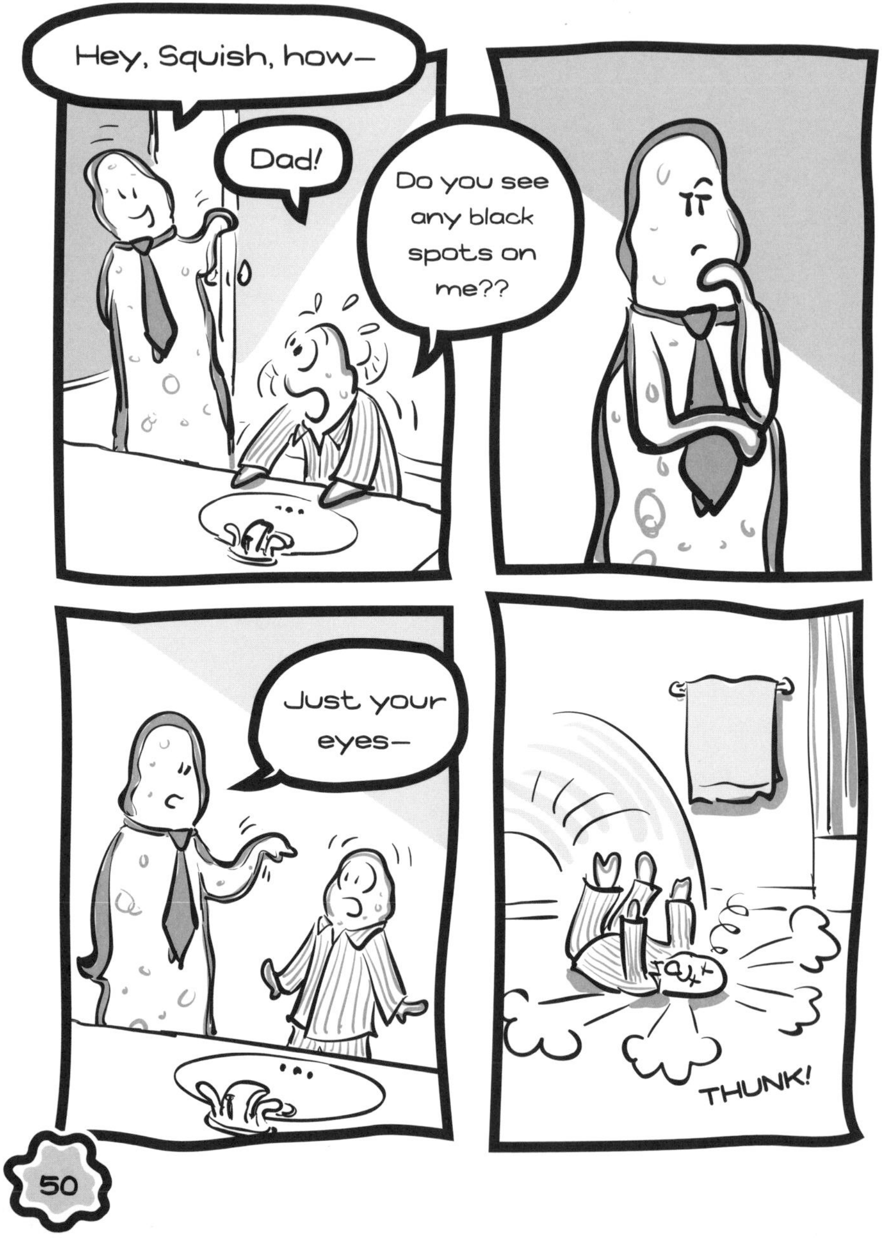
Hey, Squish, how—
Dad!
Do you see any black spots on me??
Just your eyes—
THUNK!

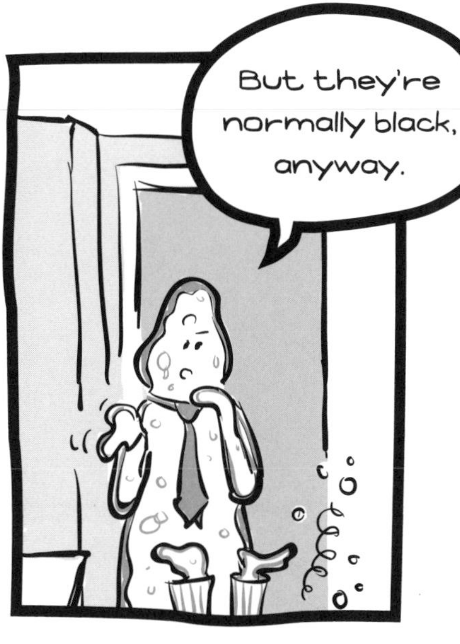
But they're normally black, anyway.

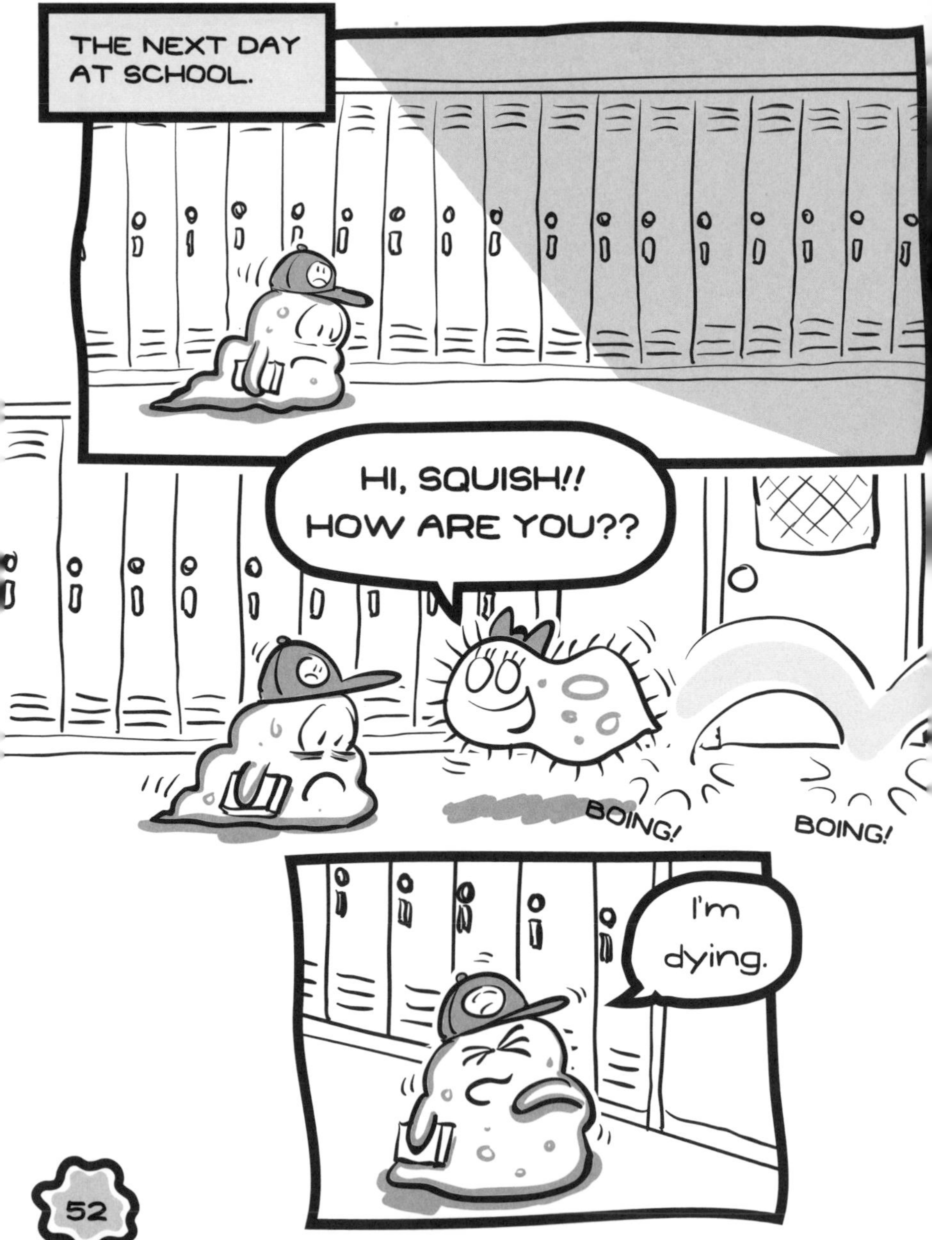
THE NEXT DAY AT SCHOOL.
HI, SQUISH!! HOW ARE YOU??
BOING!
BOING!
I'm dying.

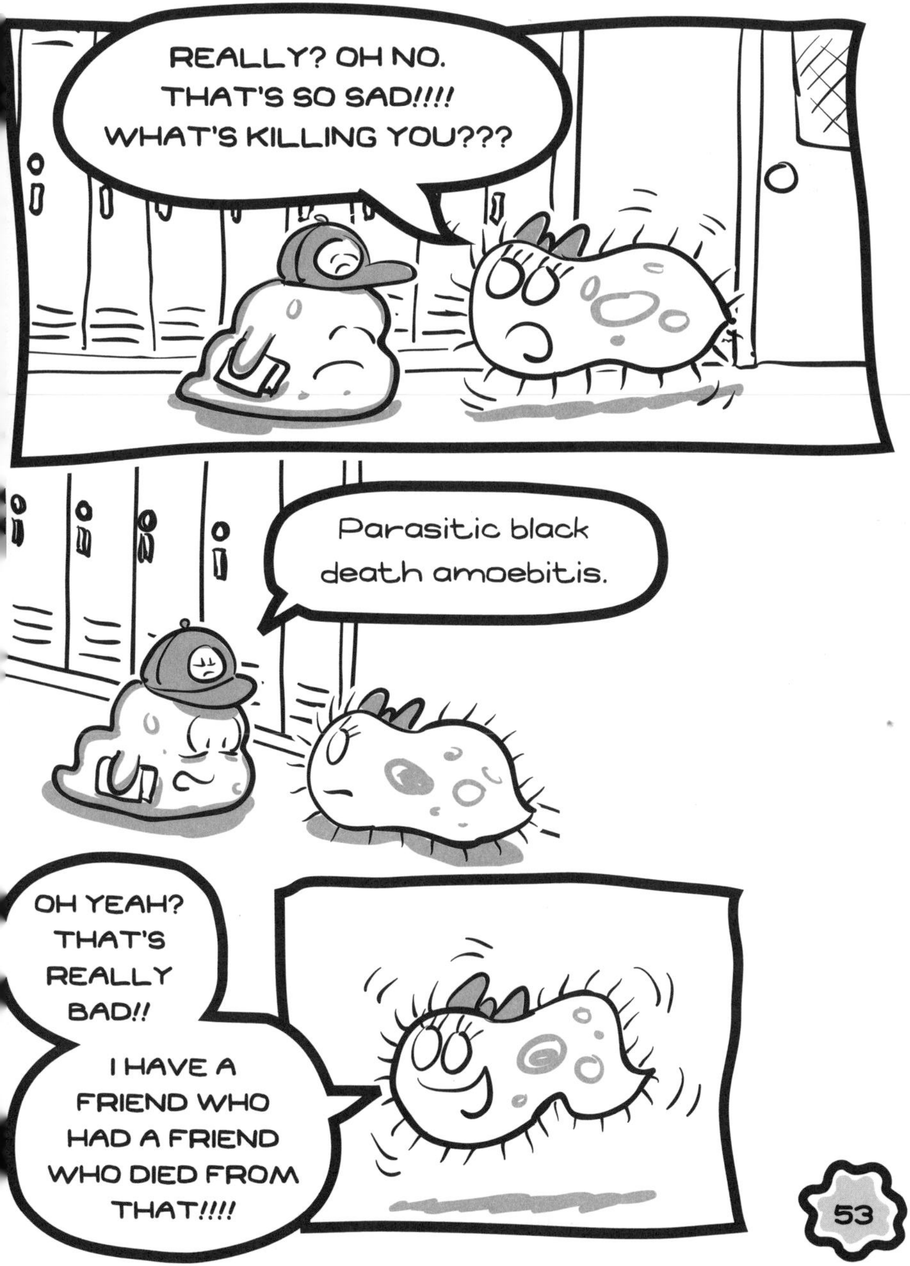
REALLY? OH NO. THAT'S SO SAD!!!! WHAT'S KILLING YOU???
Parasitic black death amoebitis.
OH YEAH? THAT'S REALLY BAD!!
I HAVE A FRIEND WHO HAD A FRIEND WHO DIED FROM THAT!!!!

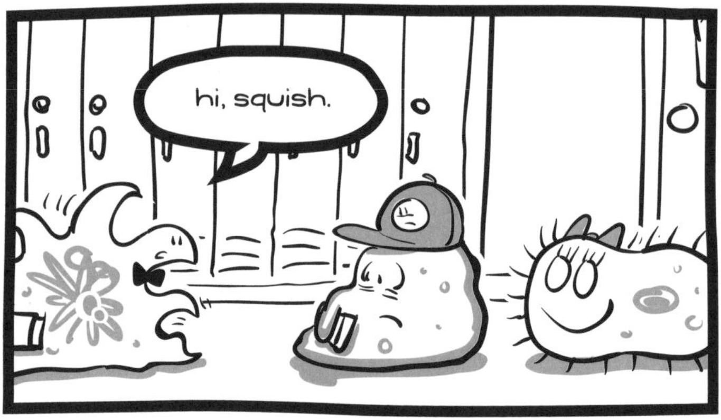
hi, squish.

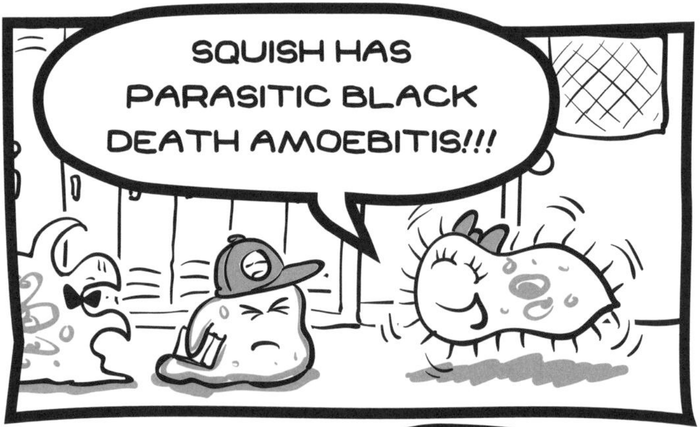
SQUISH HAS PARASITIC BLACK DEATH AMOEBITIS!!!

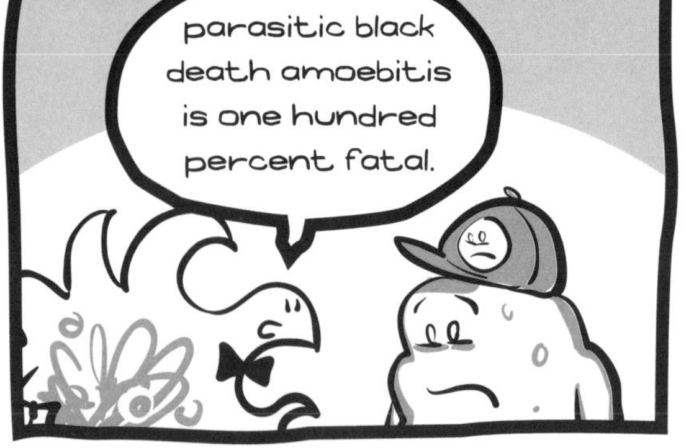
parasitic black death amoebitis is one hundred percent fatal.

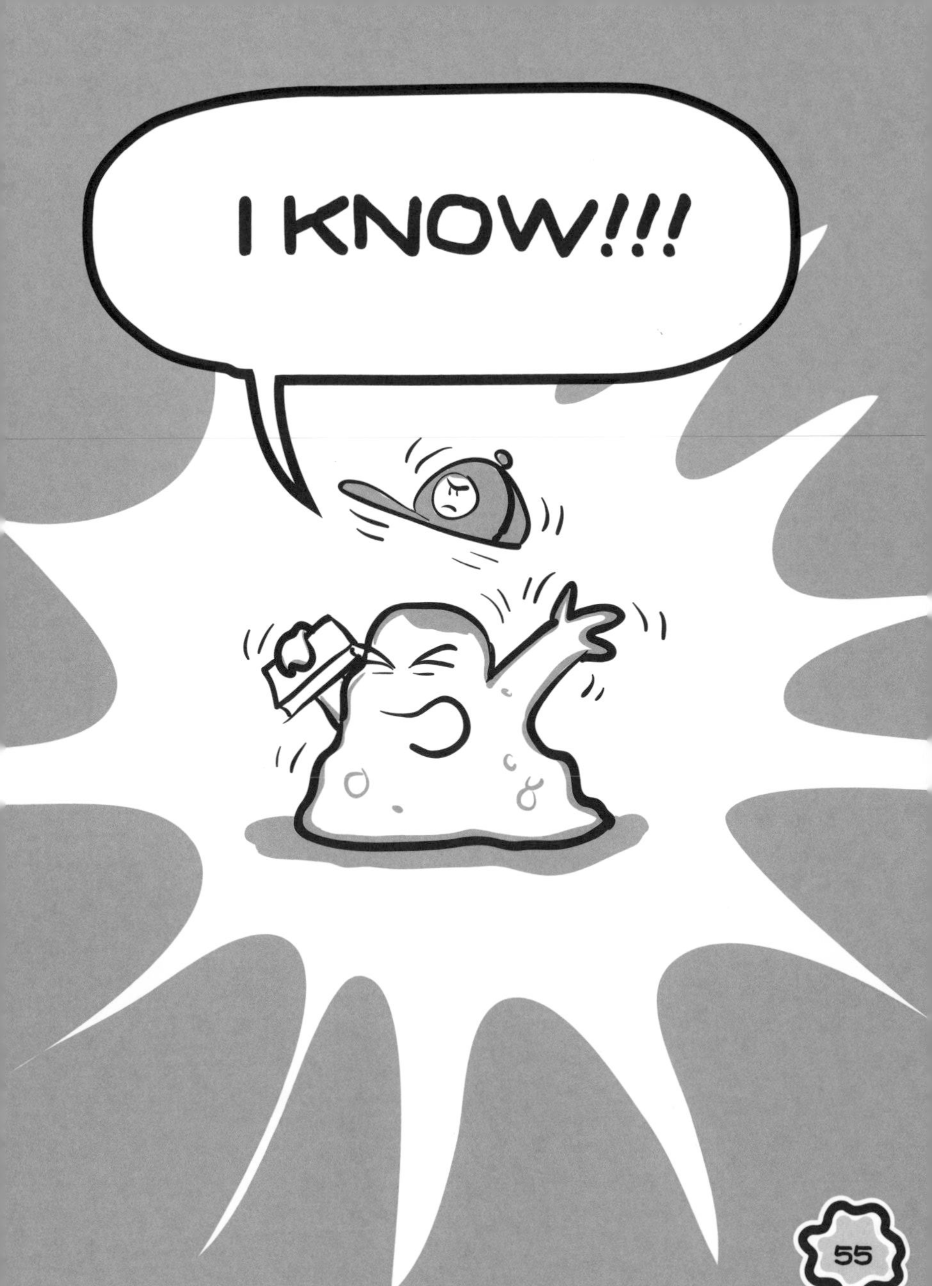
I KNOW!!!

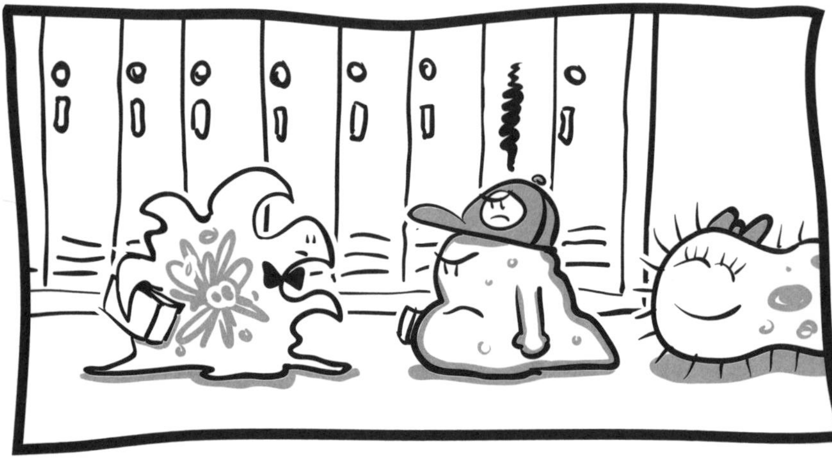

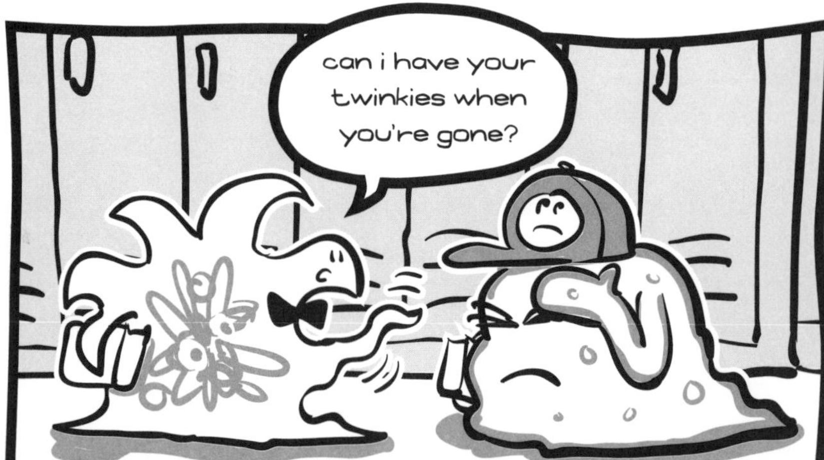
can i have your twinkies when you're gone?

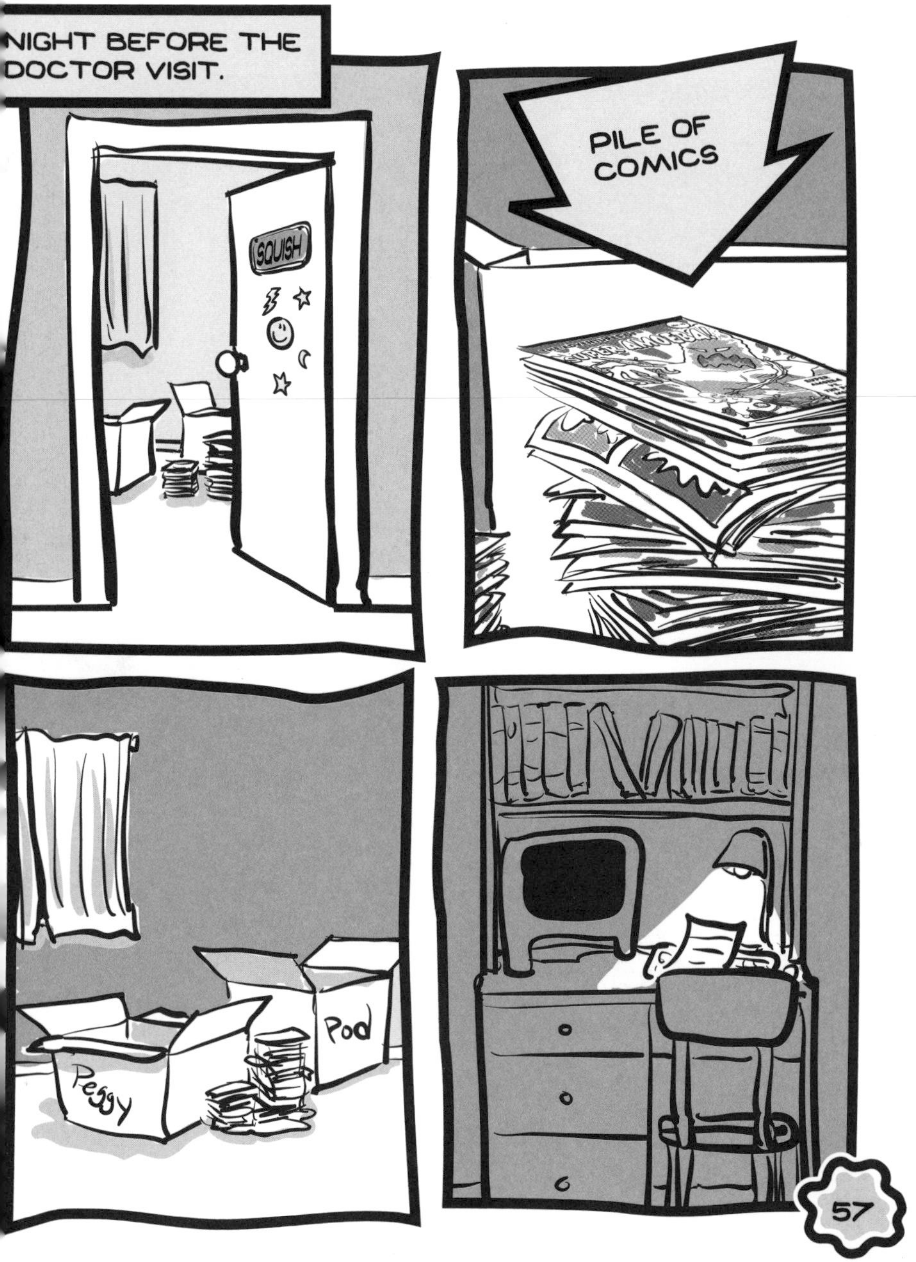
NIGHT BEFORE THE DOCTOR VISIT.
SQUISH
PILE OF COMICS
Peggy
Pod

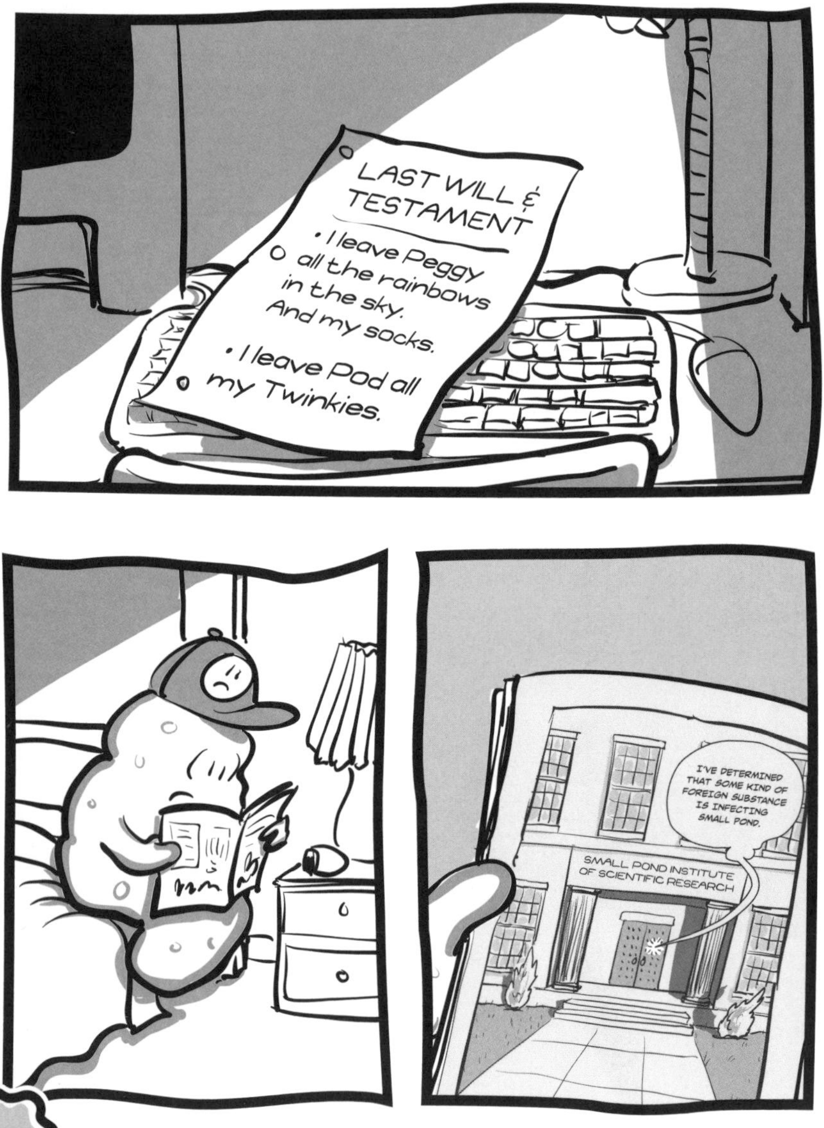
LAST WILL & TESTAMENT
• I leave Peggy all the rainbows in the sky. And my socks.
• I leave Pod all my Twinkies.
SMALL POND INSTITUTE OF SCIENTIFIC RESEARCH
I'VE DETERMINED THAT SOME KIND OF FOREIGN SUBSTANCE IS INFECTING SMALL POND.

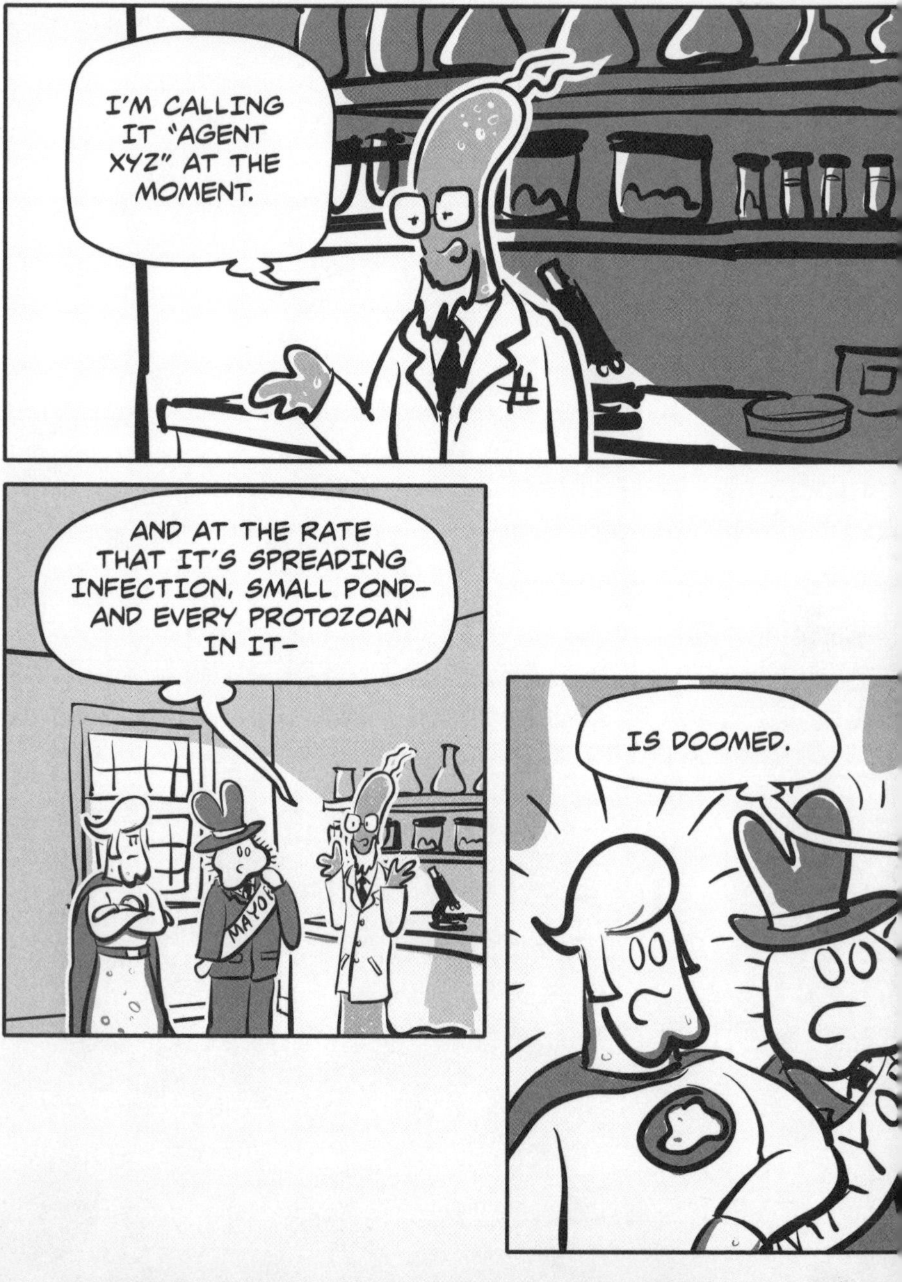
I'M CALLING IT "AGENT XYZ" AT THE MOMENT.
AND AT THE RATE THAT IT'S SPREADING INFECTION, SMALL POND-AND EVERY PROTOZOAN IN IT-
MAYOR
IS DOOMED.

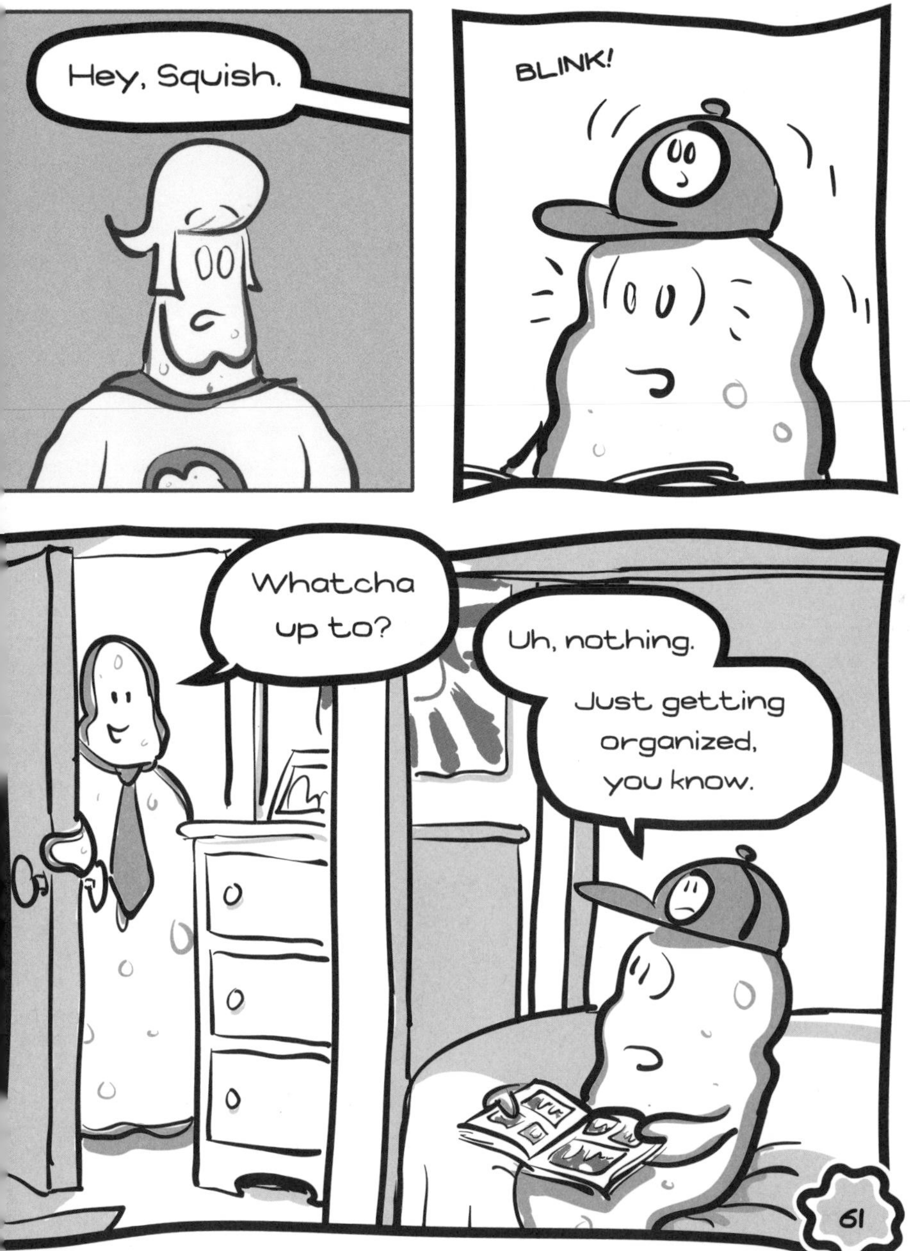
Hey, Squish.
BLINK!
Whatcha up to?
Uh, nothing.
Just getting organized, you know.

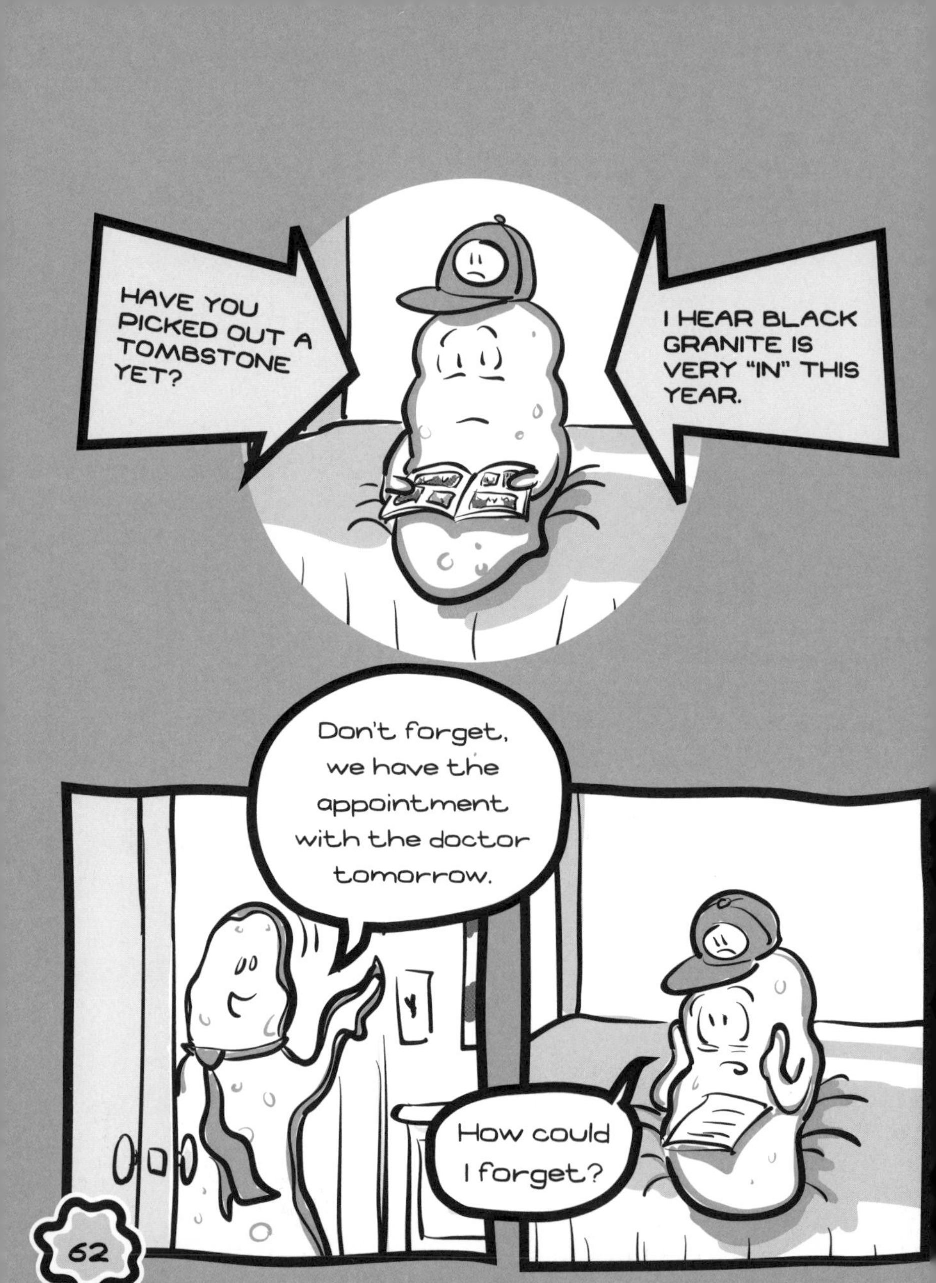

HAVE YOU PICKED OUT A TOMBSTONE YET?
I HEAR BLACK GRANITE IS VERY "IN" THIS YEAR.
Don't forget, we have the appointment with the doctor tomorrow.
How could I forget?

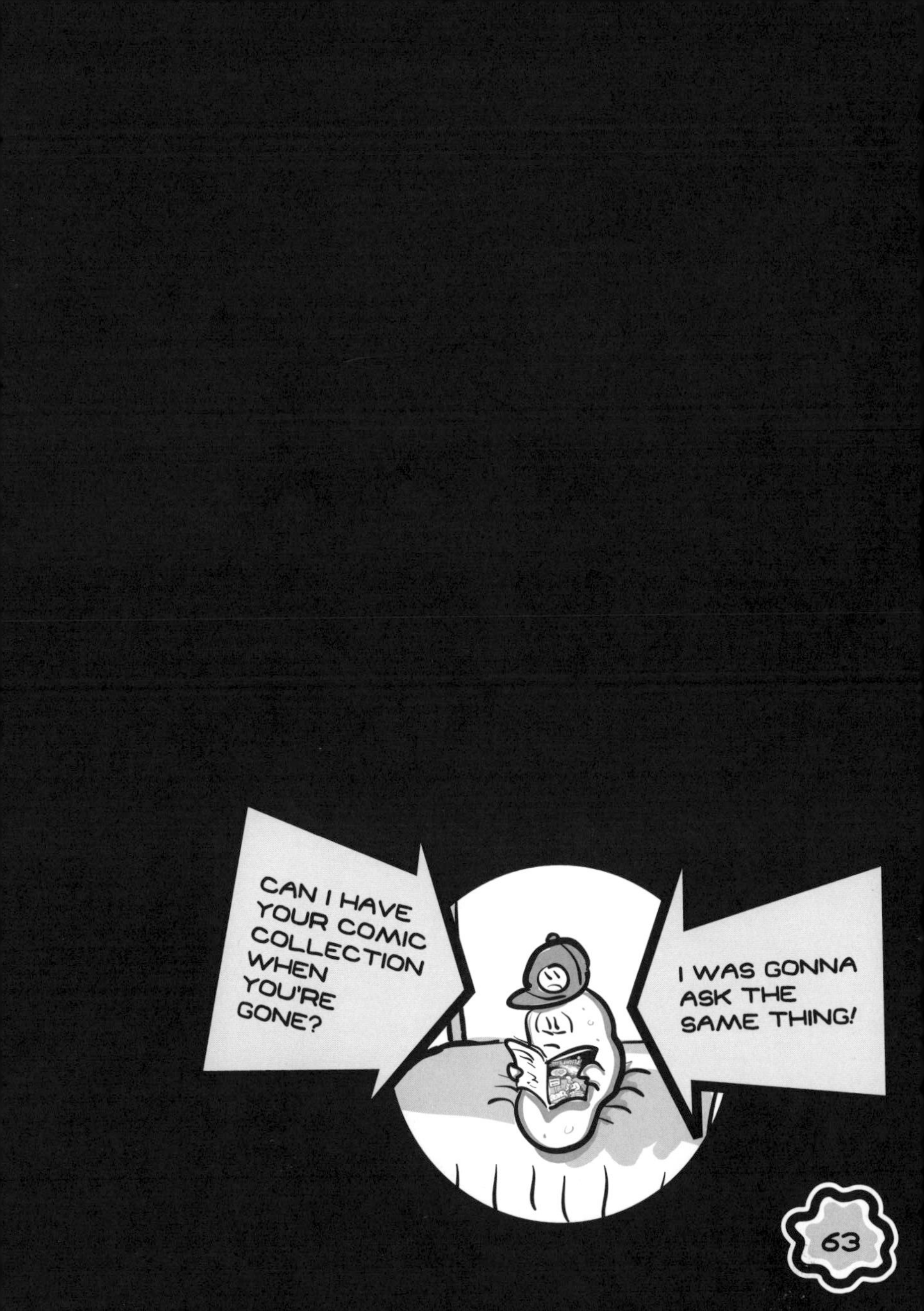
CAN I HAVE YOUR COMIC COLLECTION WHEN YOU'RE GONE?
I WAS GONNA ASK THE SAME THING!

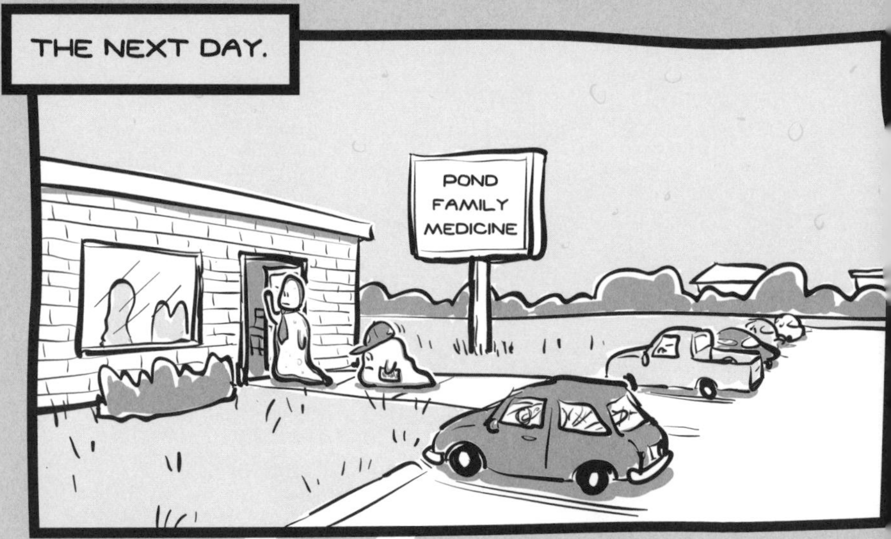
THE NEXT DAY.
POND
FAMILY
MEDICINE

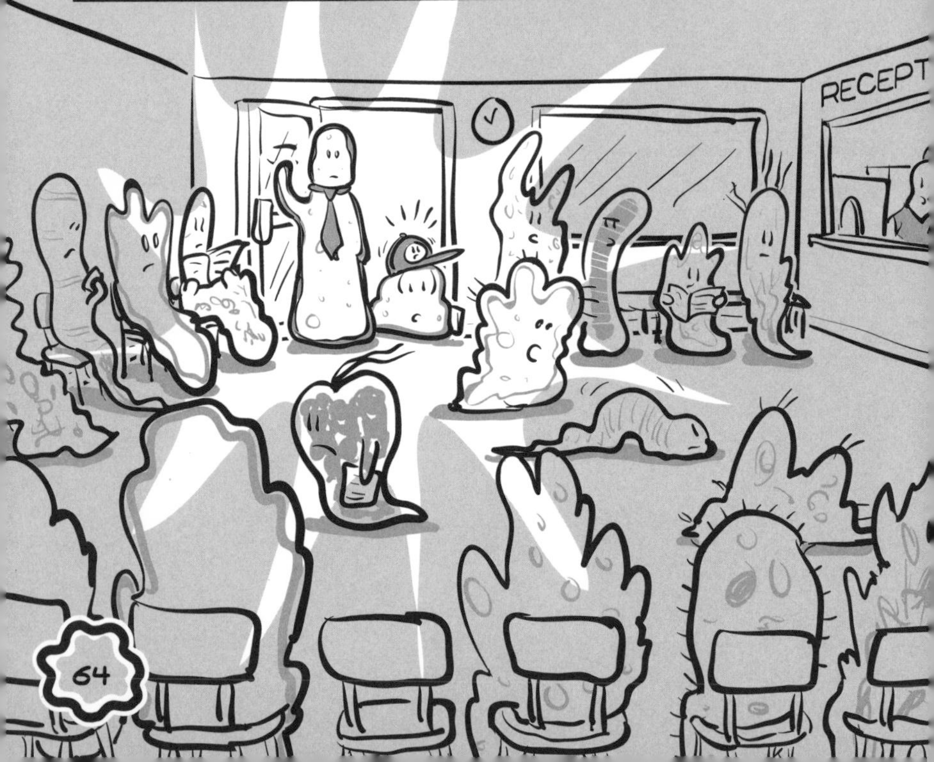
RECEPT

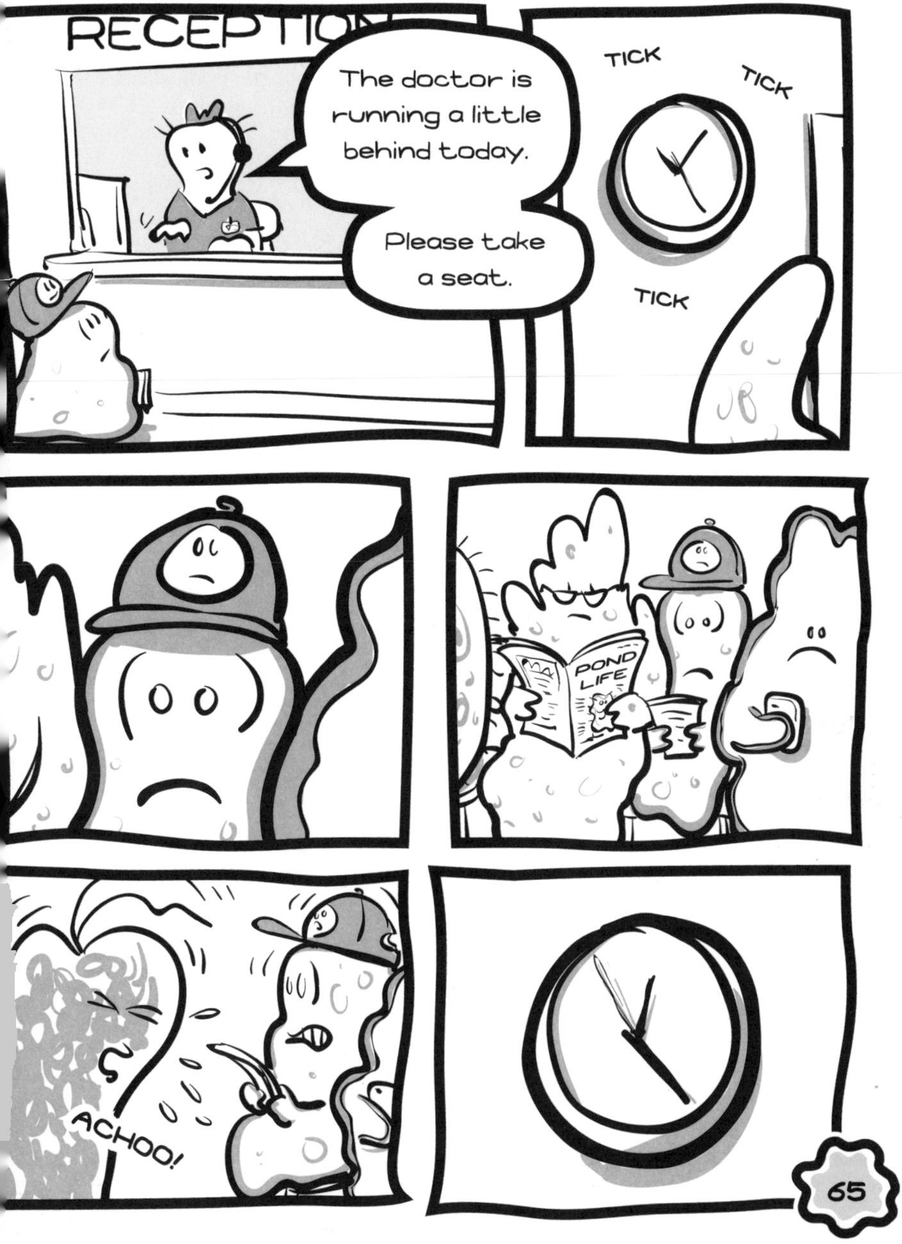
RECEPTION
The doctor is running a little behind today.
Please take a seat.
TICK
TICK
TICK
POND LIFE
ACHOO!

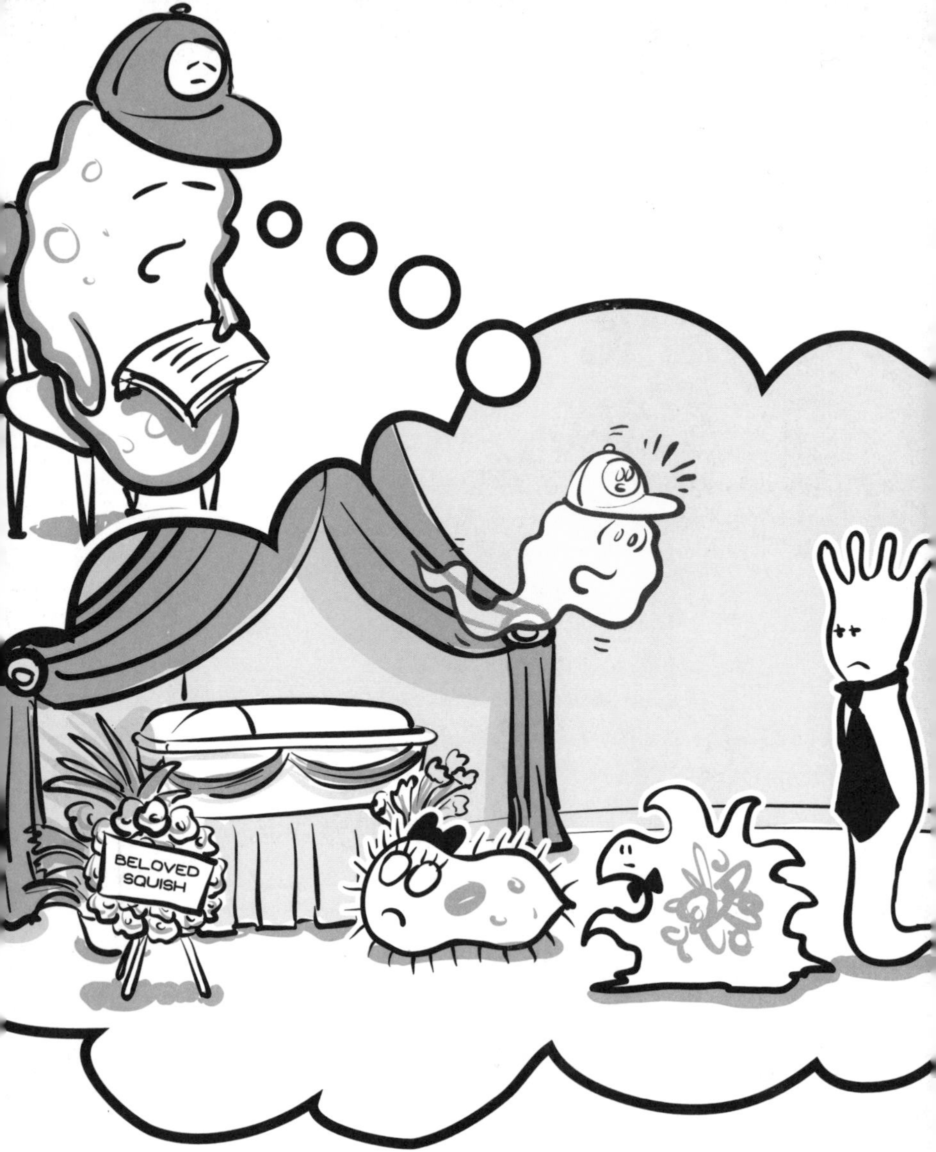
BELOVED
SQUISH

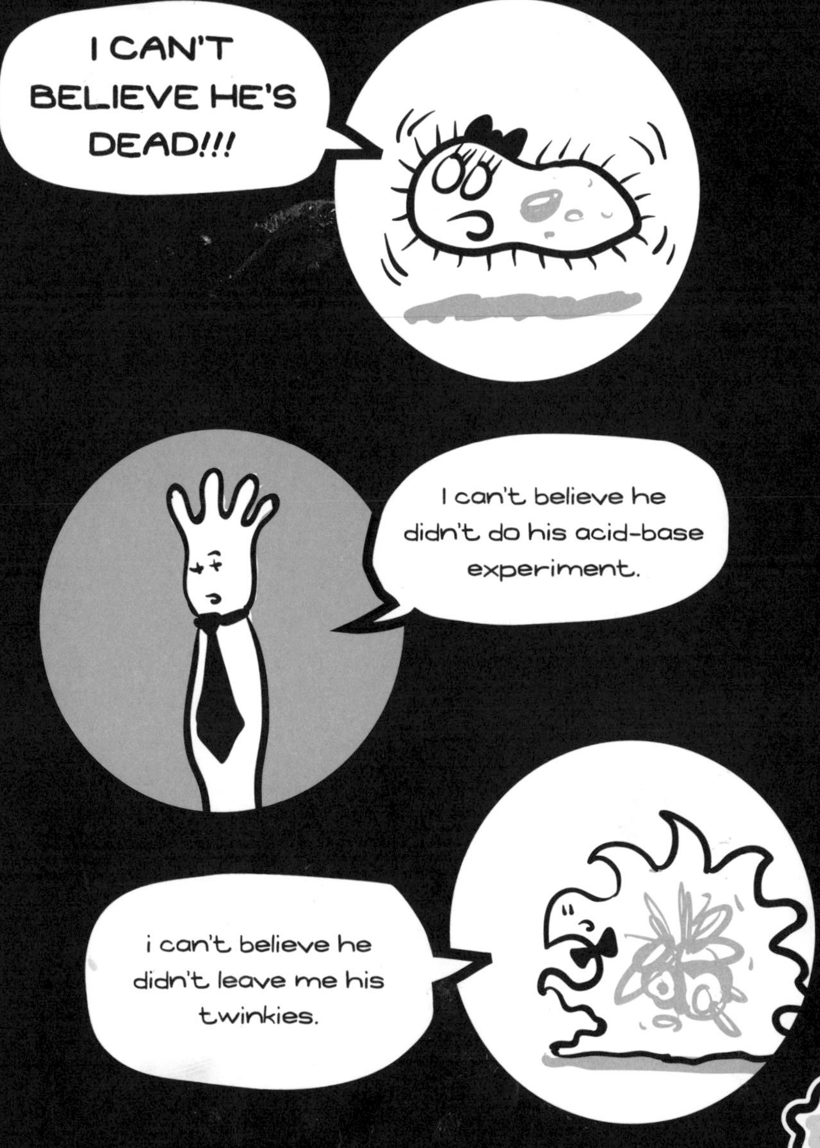
I CAN'T BELIEVE HE'S DEAD!!!
I can't believe he didn't do his acid-base experiment.
i can't believe he didn't leave me his twinkies.

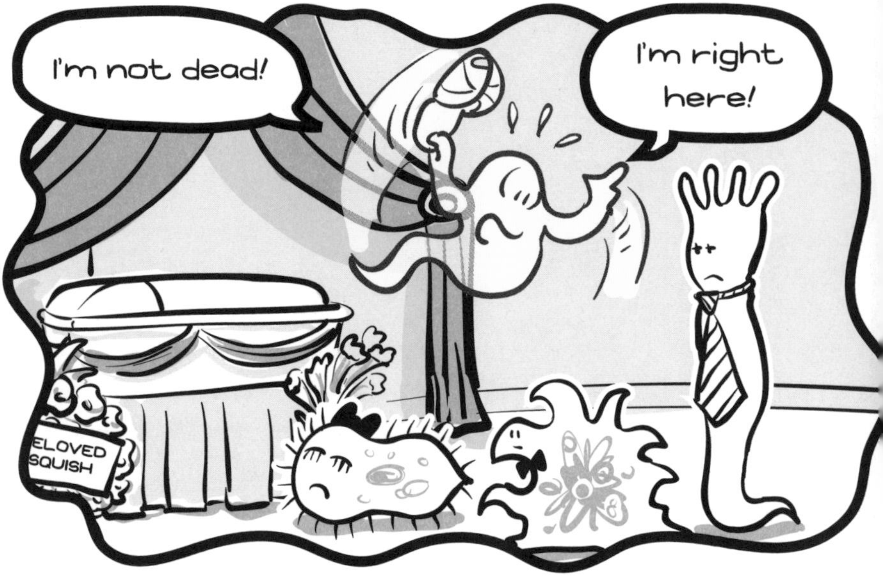
I'm not dead!
I'm right here!
ELOVED SQUISH

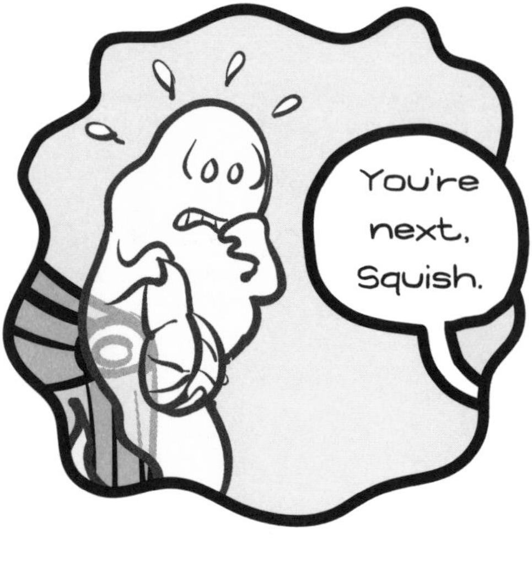
You're next, Squish.

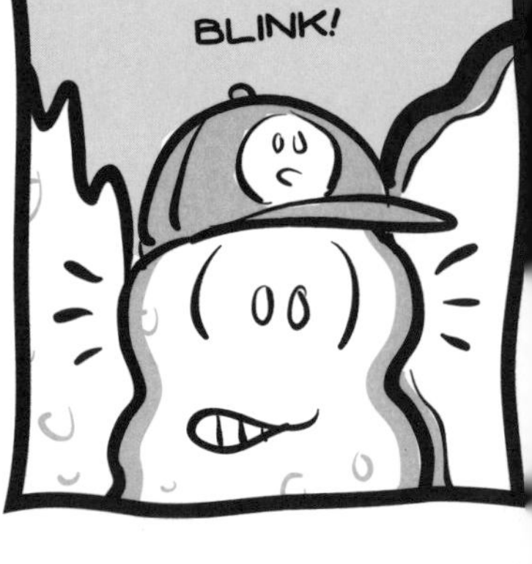
BLINK!

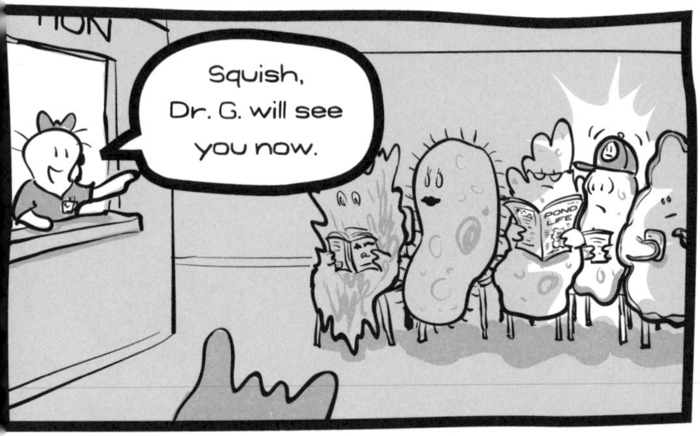
Squish,
Dr. G. will see
you now.
POND
LIFE

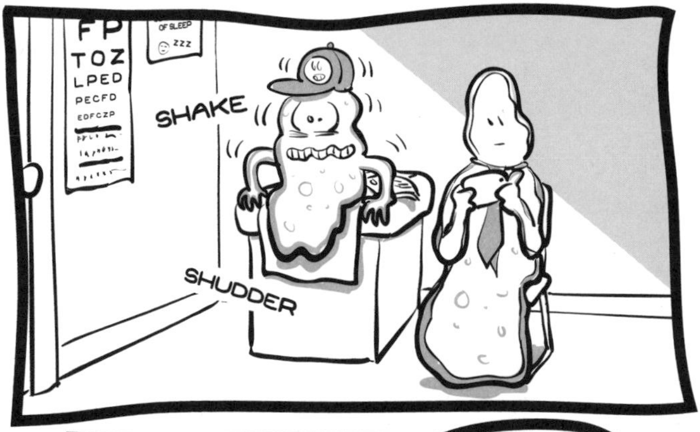
F P
TOZ
LPED
PECFD
EDFCZP
OF SLEEP
SHAKE
SHUDDER

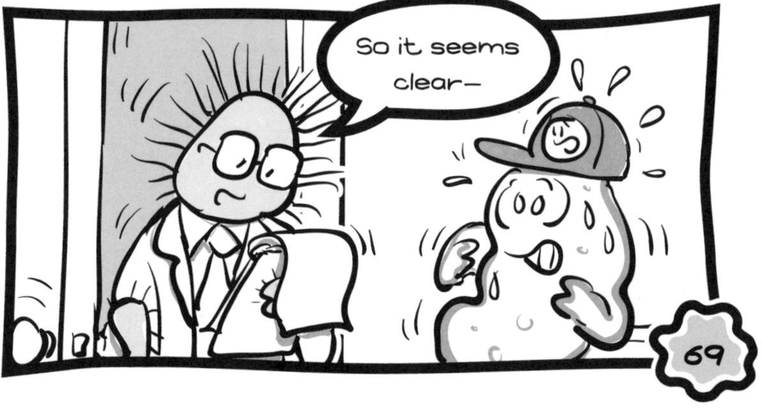
So it seems
clear—

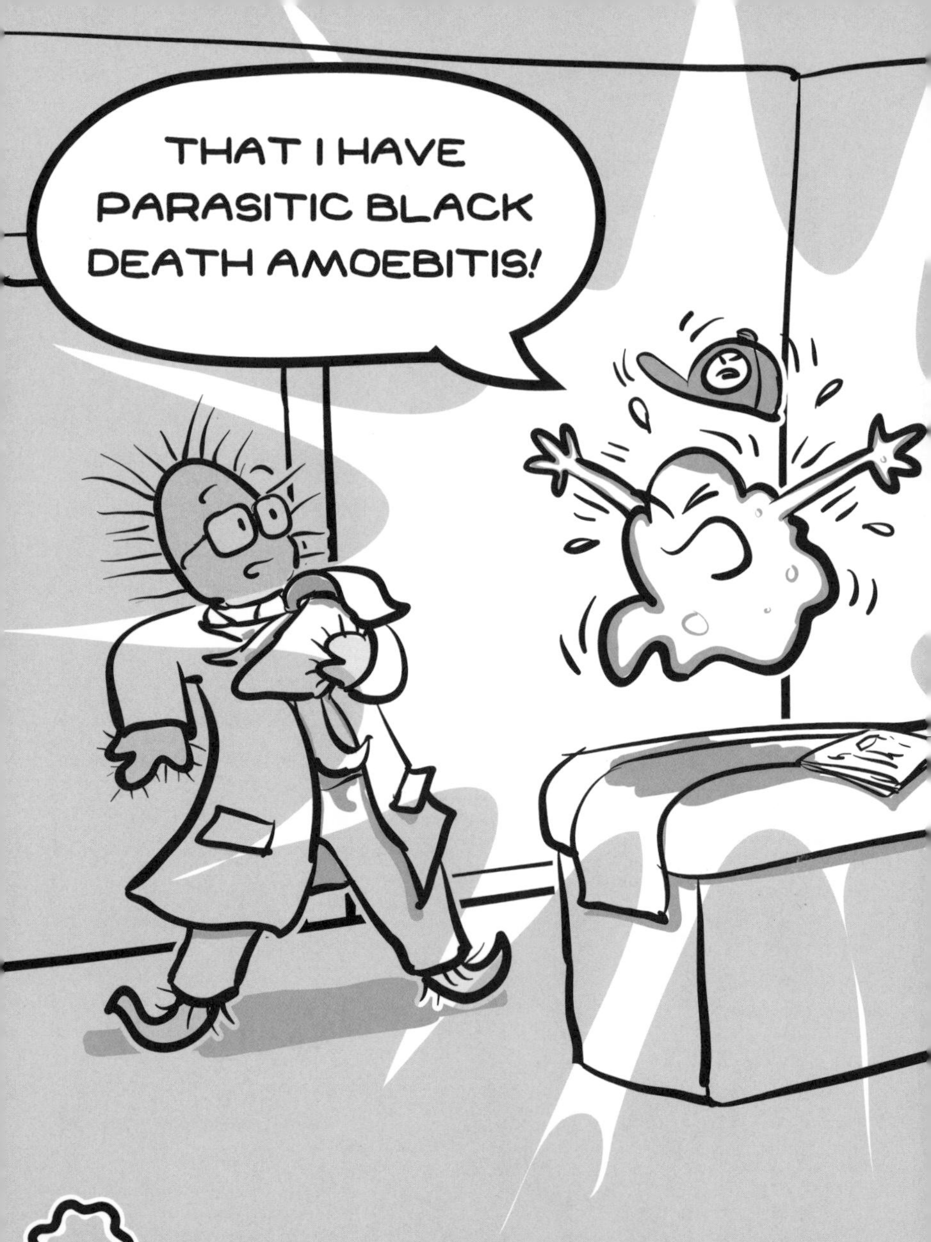
THAT I HAVE PARASITIC BLACK DEATH AMOEBITIS!

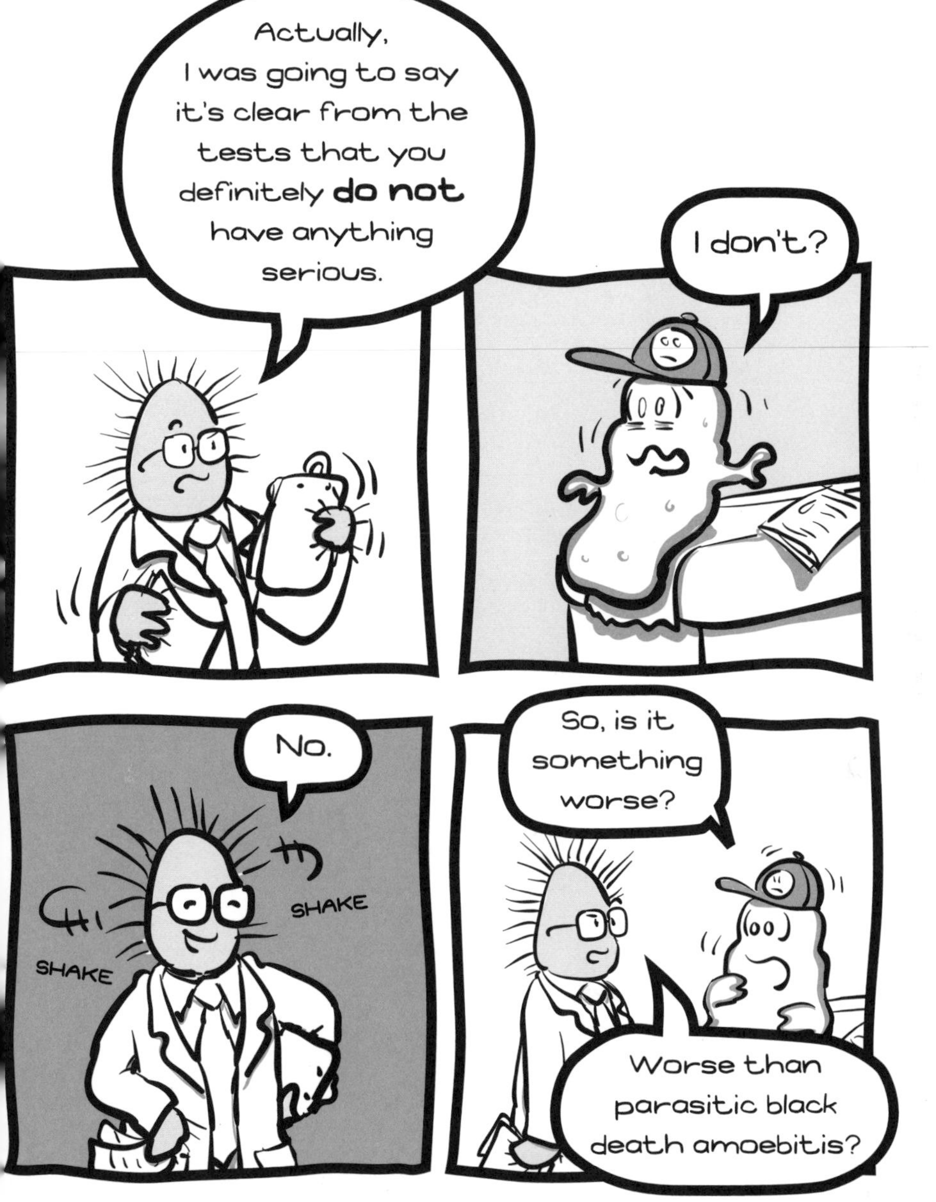
Actually, I was going to say it's clear from the tests that you definitely **do not** have anything serious.
I don't?
No.
SHAKE
SHAKE
So, is it something worse?
Worse than parasitic black death amoebitis?

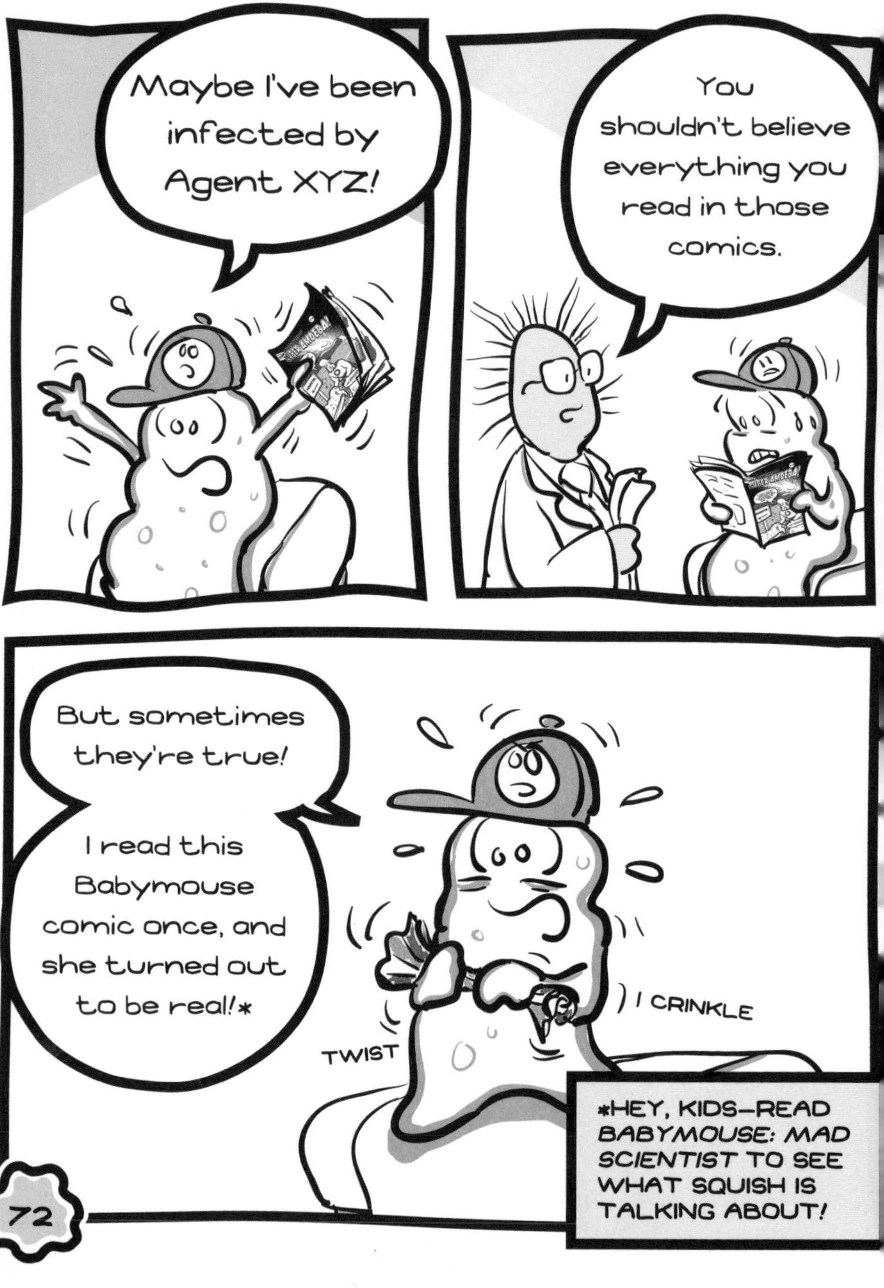
Maybe I've been infected by Agent XYZ!
SUPER AMOEBA!
You shouldn't believe everything you read in those comics.
SUPER AMOEBA
But sometimes they're true!
I read this Babymouse comic once, and she turned out to be real!*
TWIST
CRINKLE
*HEY, KIDS—READ BABYMOUSE: MAD SCIENTIST TO SEE WHAT SQUISH IS TALKING ABOUT!

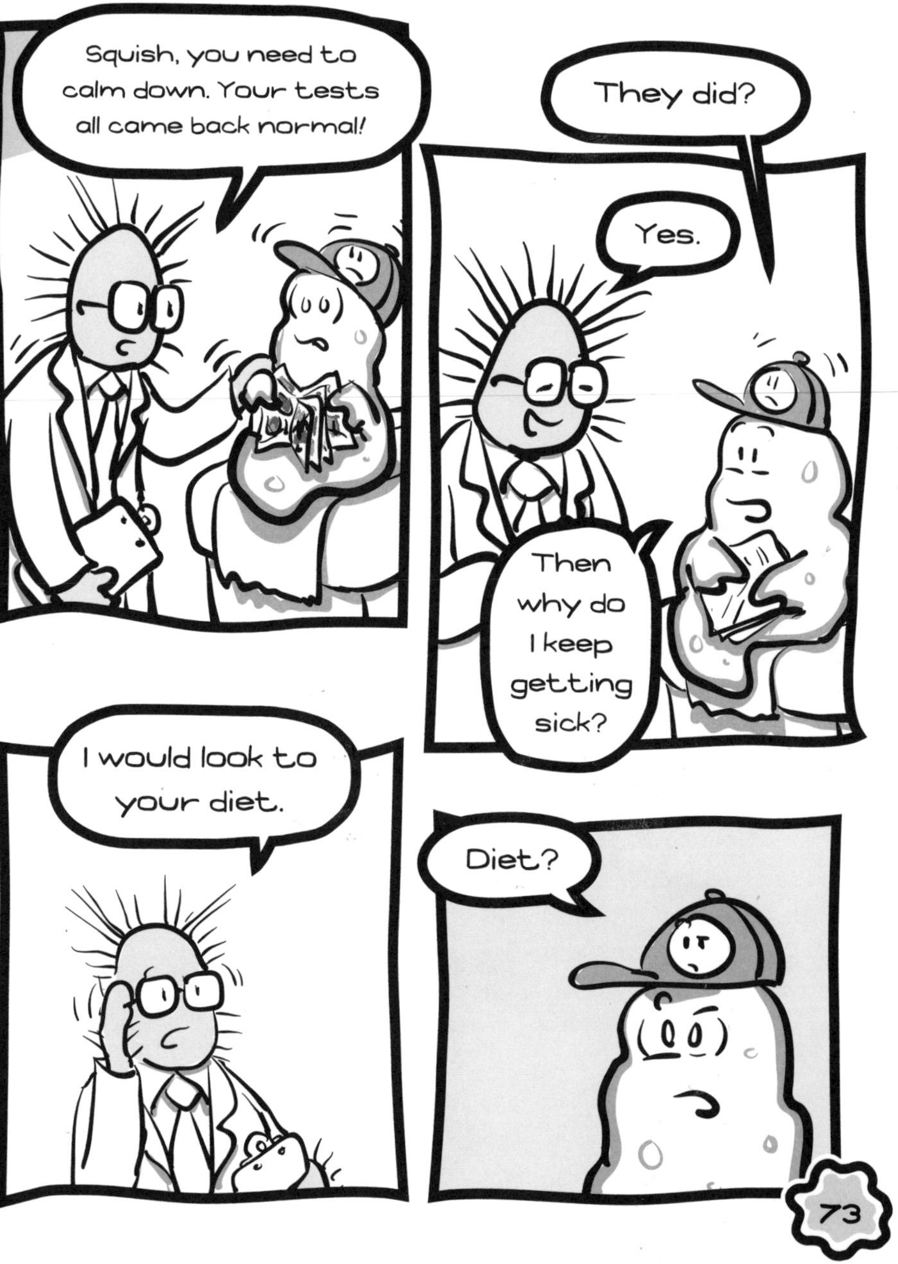
Squish, you need to calm down. Your tests all came back normal!
They did?
Yes.
Then why do I keep getting sick?
I would look to your diet.
Diet?

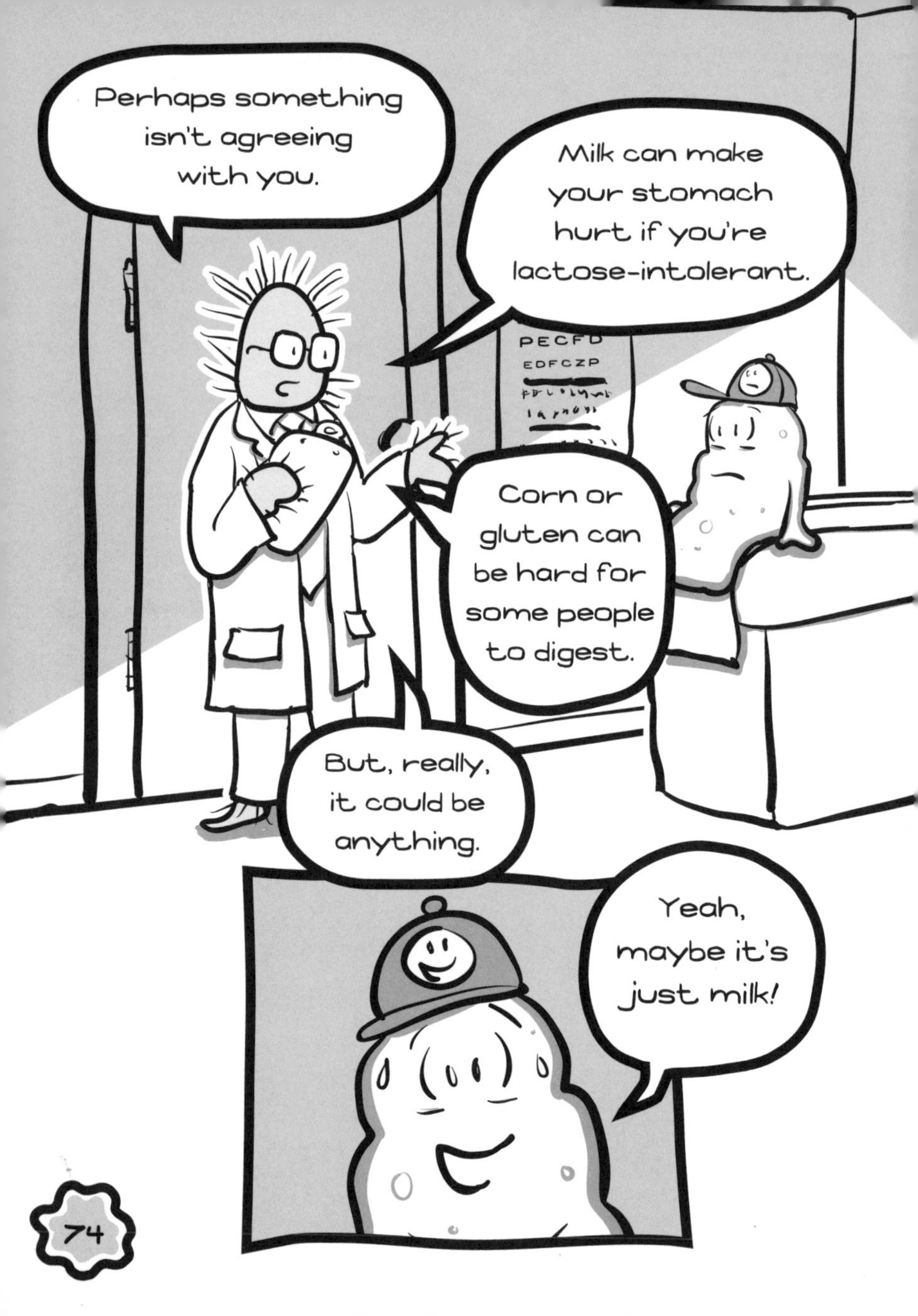
Perhaps something isn't agreeing with you.
Milk can make your stomach hurt if you're lactose-intolerant.
Corn or gluten can be hard for some people to digest.
But, really, it could be anything.
Yeah, maybe it's just milk!

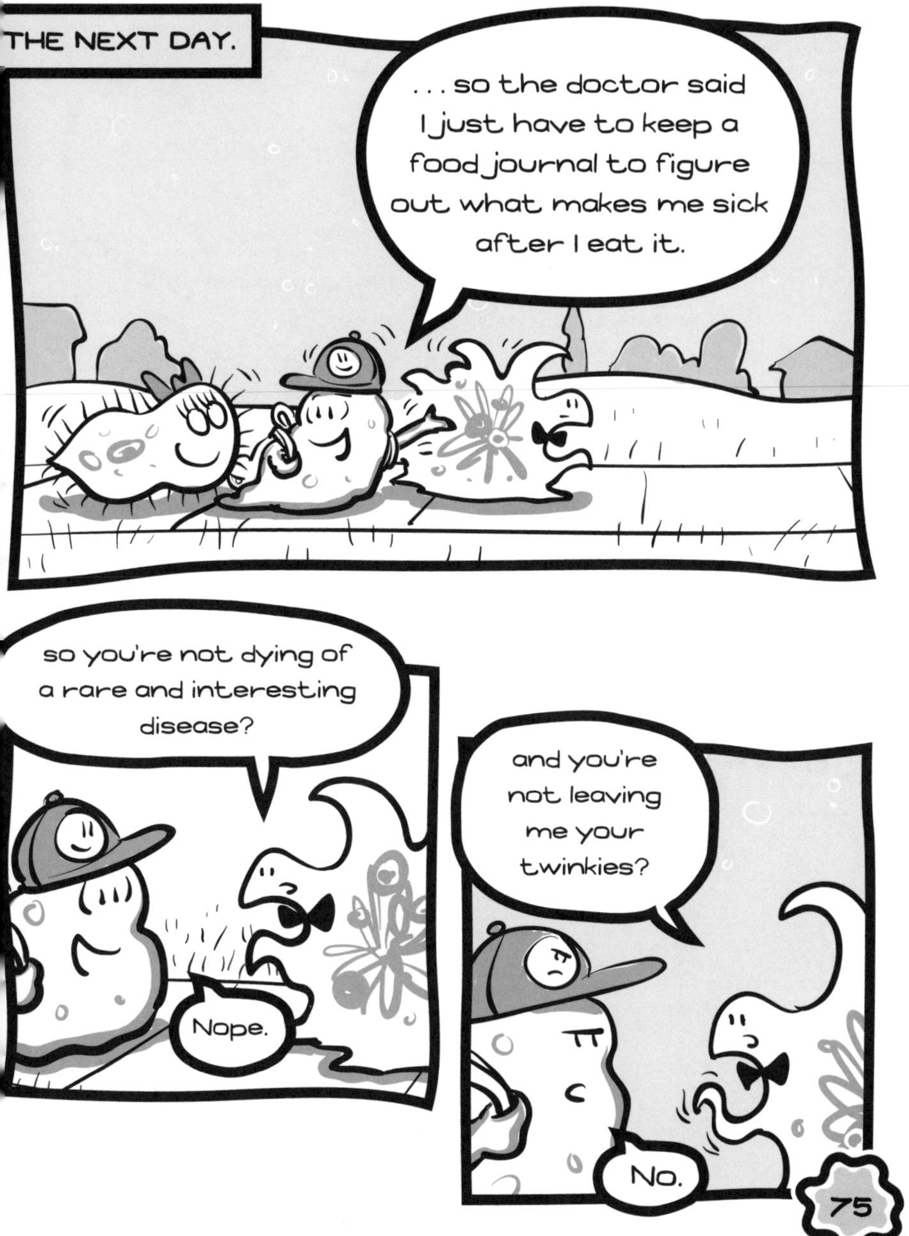
THE NEXT DAY.
. . . so the doctor said I just have to keep a food journal to figure out what makes me sick after I eat it.
so you're not dying of a rare and interesting disease?
Nope.
and you're not leaving me your twinkies?
No.

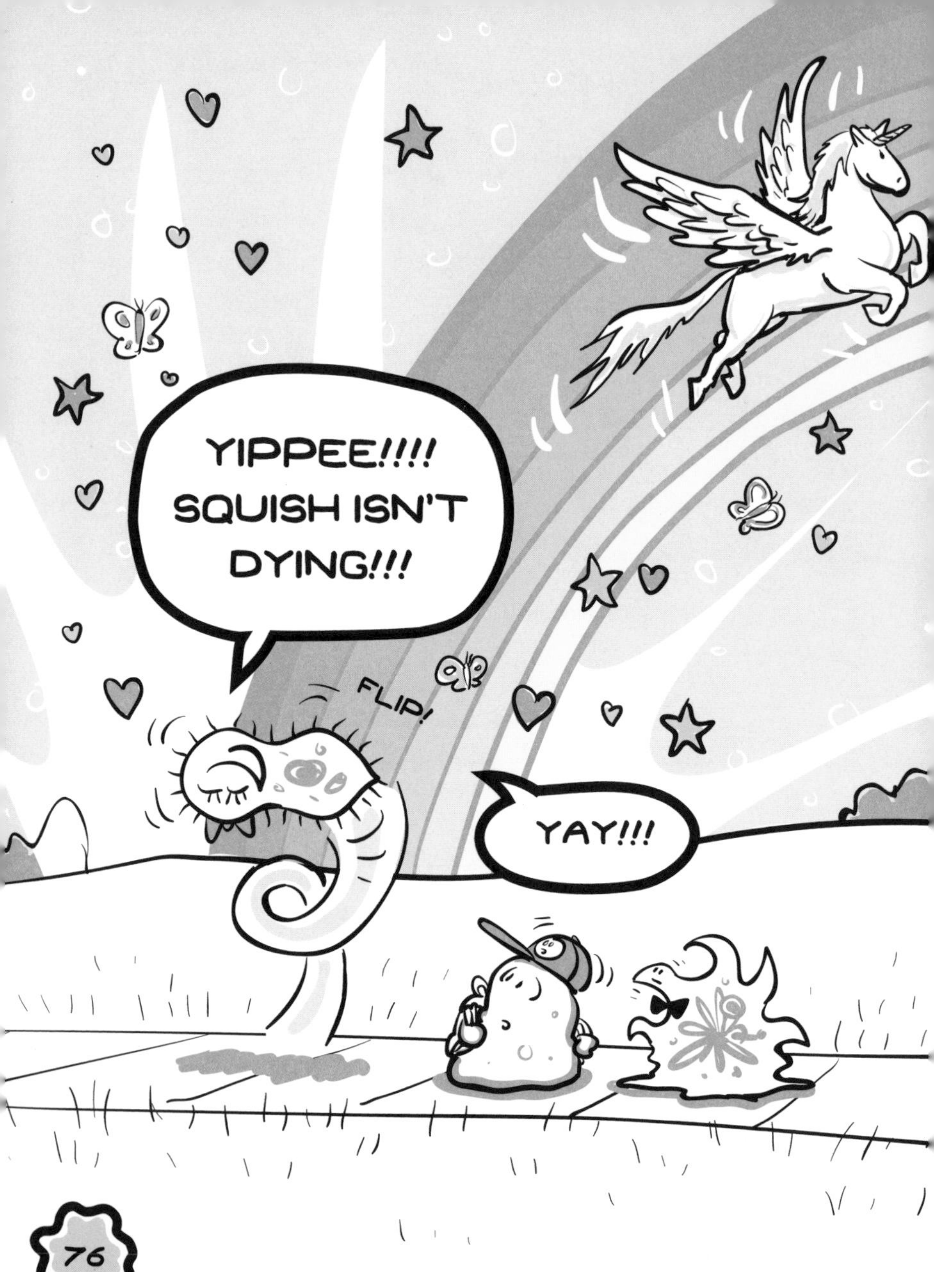
YIPPEE!!!! SQUISH ISN'T DYING!!!
FLIP!
YAY!!!

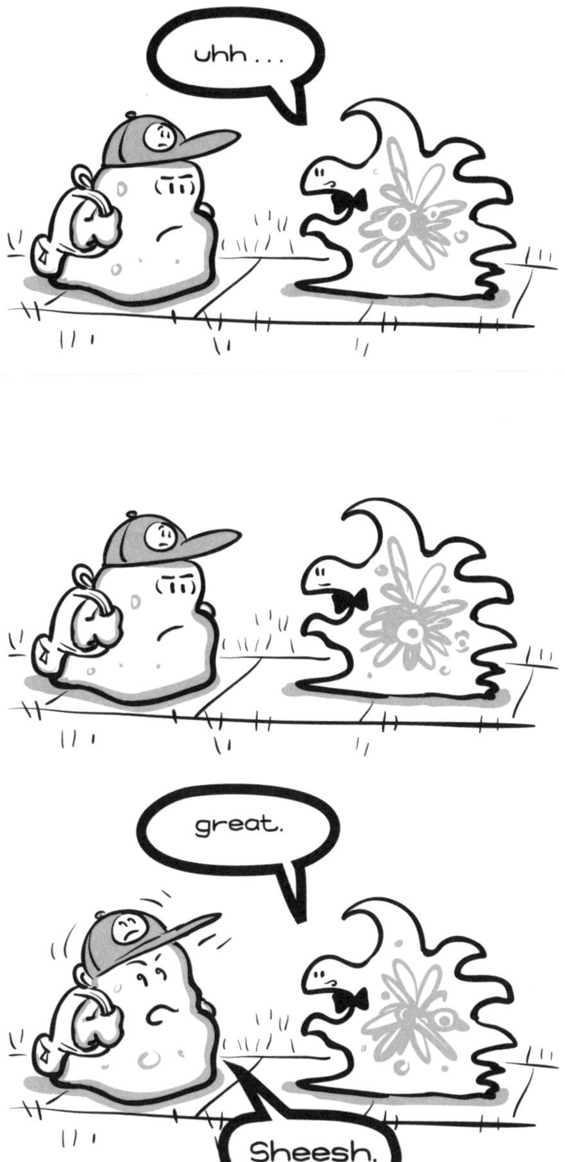
uhh . . .
great.
Sheesh.

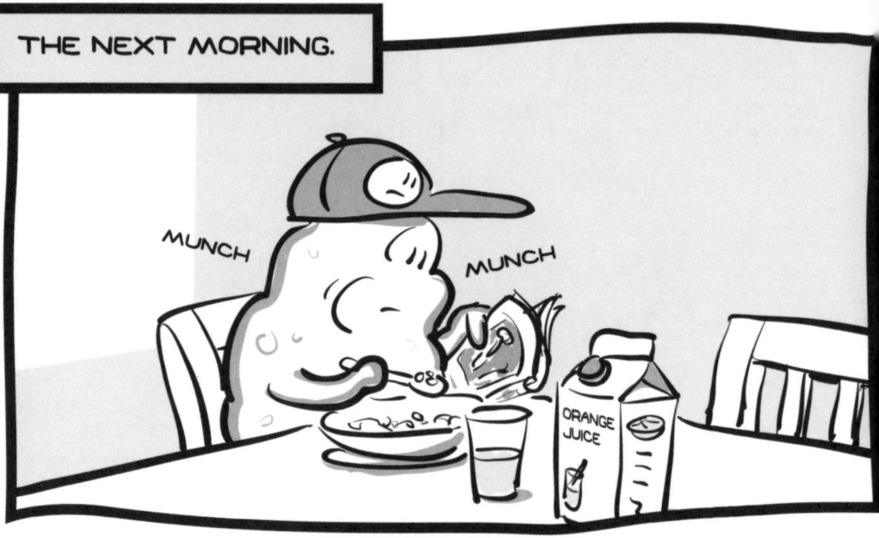
THE NEXT MORNING.
MUNCH
MUNCH
ORANGE JUICE

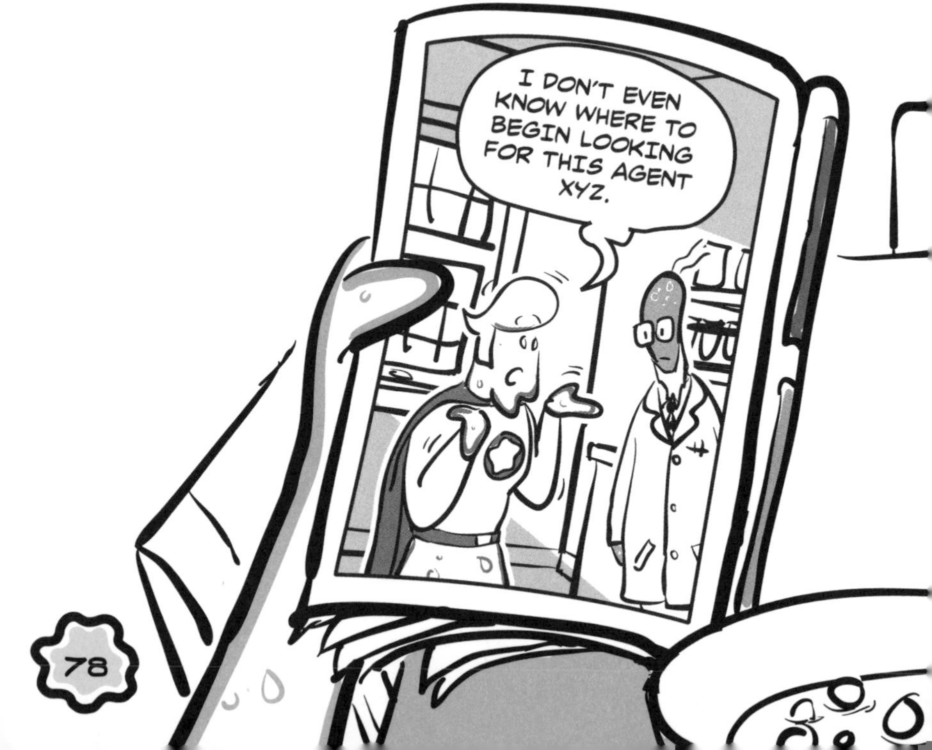
I DON'T EVEN KNOW WHERE TO BEGIN LOOKING FOR THIS AGENT XYZ.

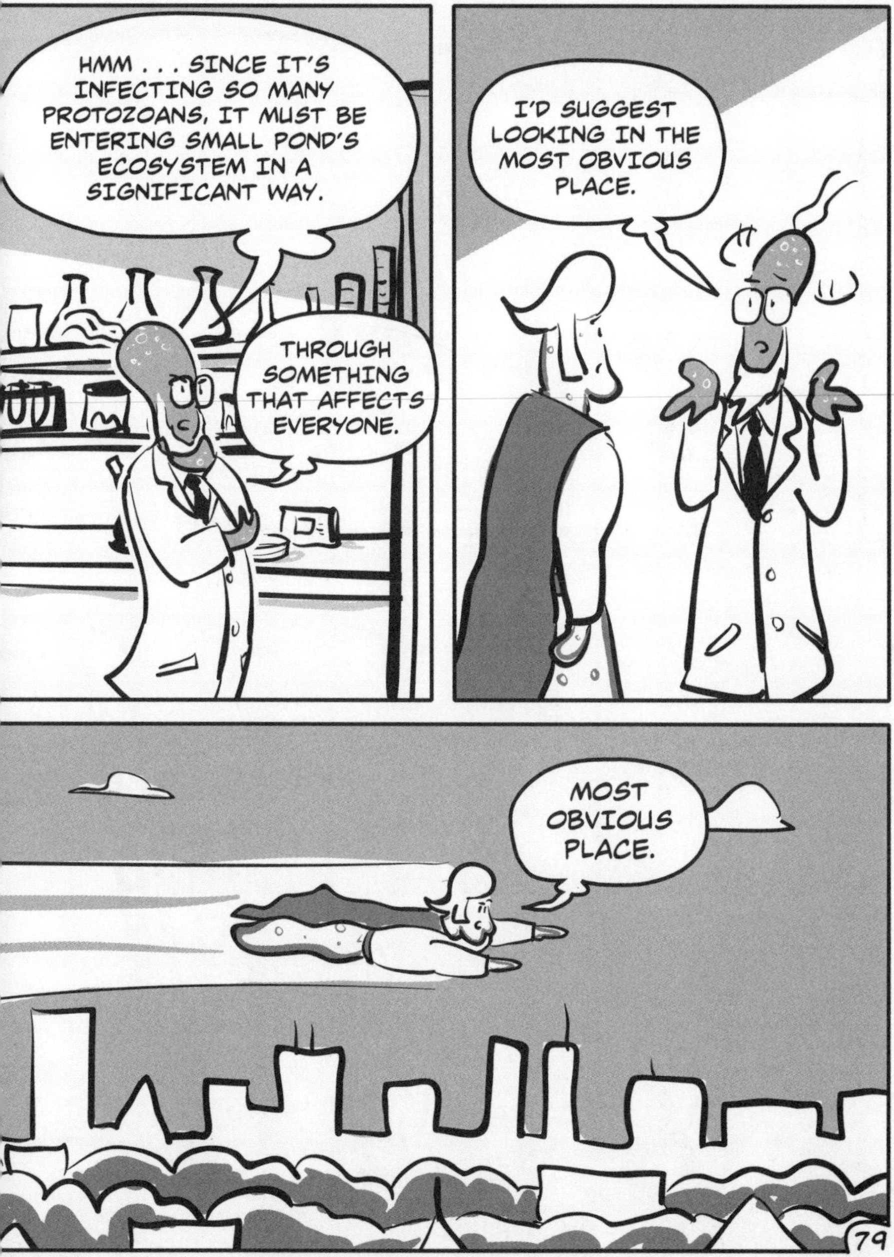
HMM . . . SINCE IT'S INFECTING SO MANY PROTOZOANS, IT MUST BE ENTERING SMALL POND'S ECOSYSTEM IN A SIGNIFICANT WAY.
THROUGH SOMETHING THAT AFFECTS EVERYONE.
I'D SUGGEST LOOKING IN THE MOST OBVIOUS PLACE.
MOST OBVIOUS PLACE.

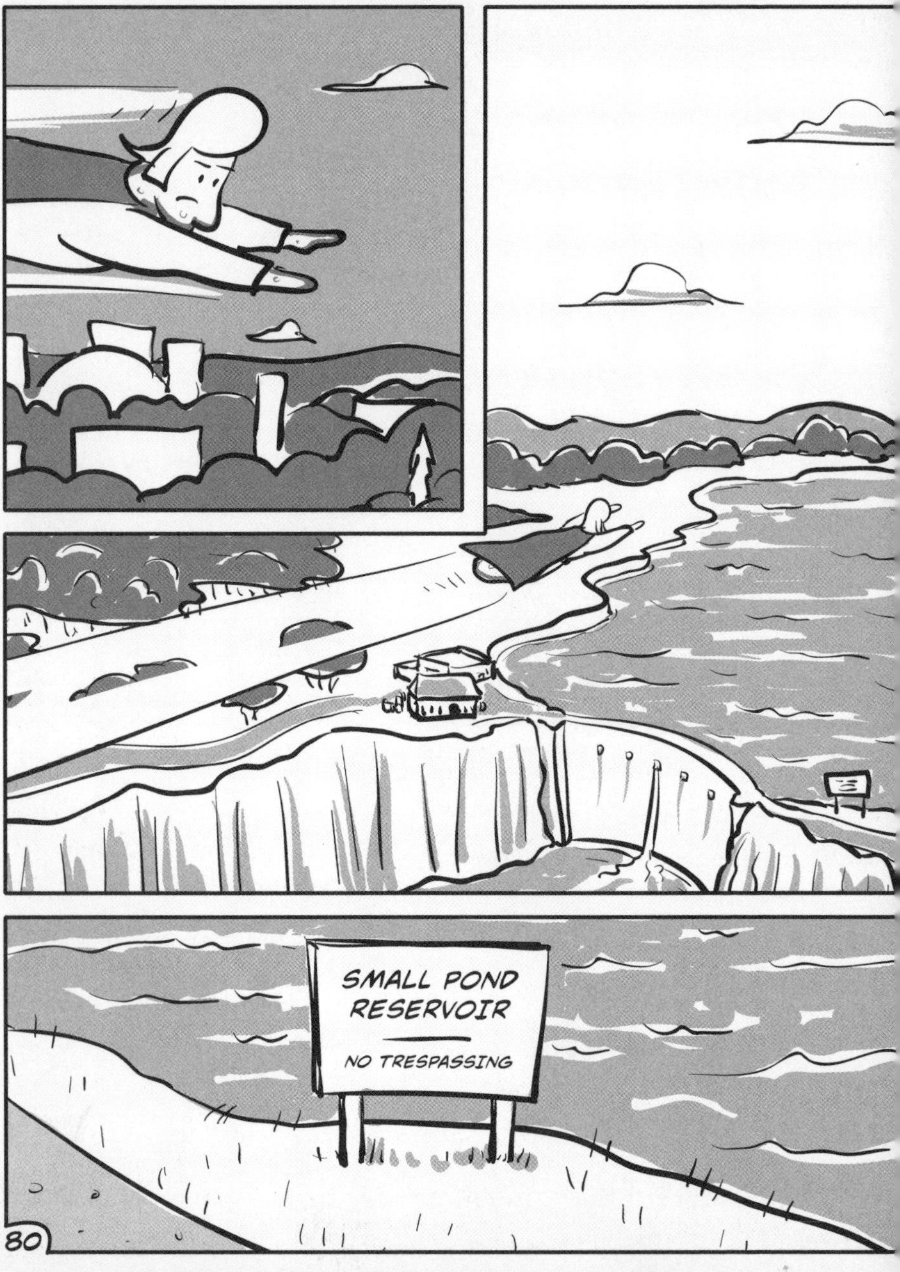
SMALL POND
RESERVOIR
NO TRESPASSING

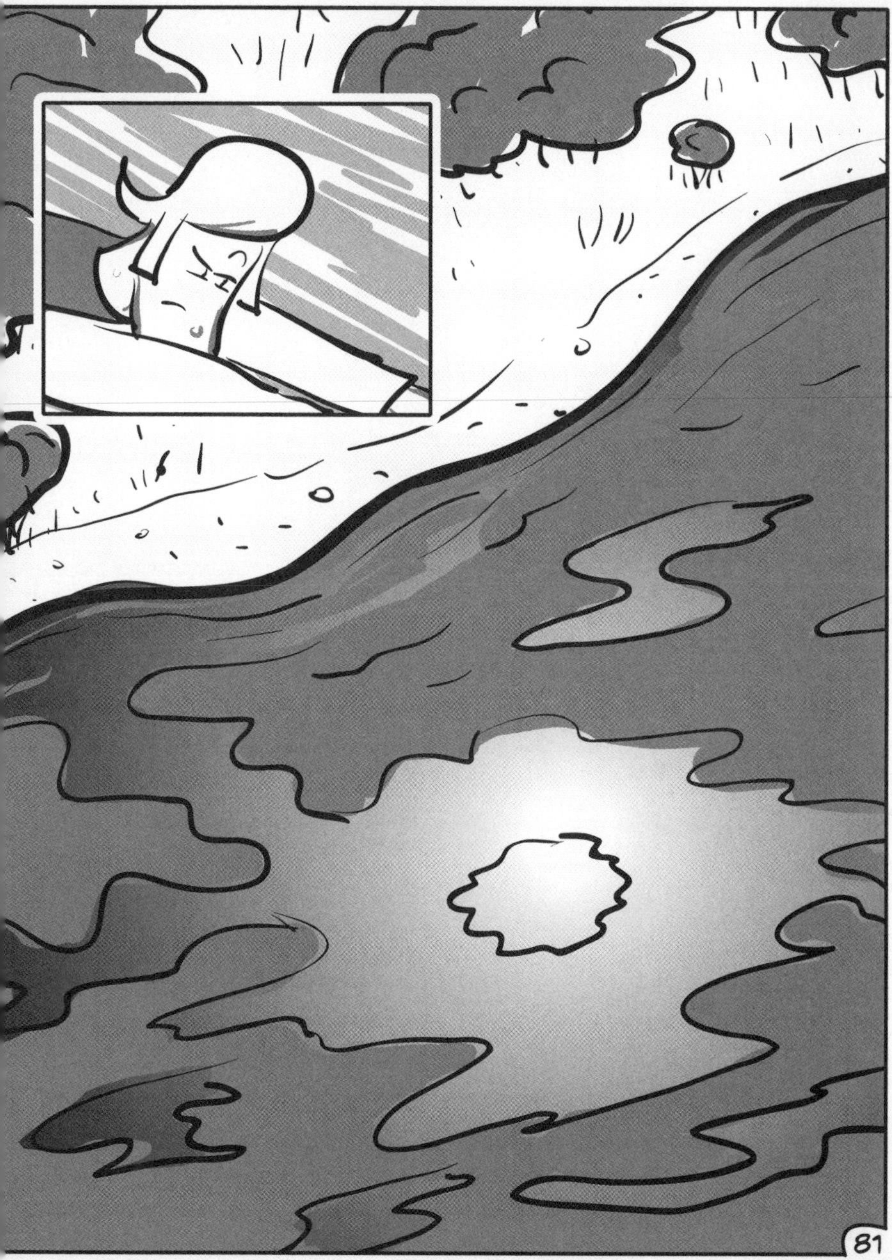

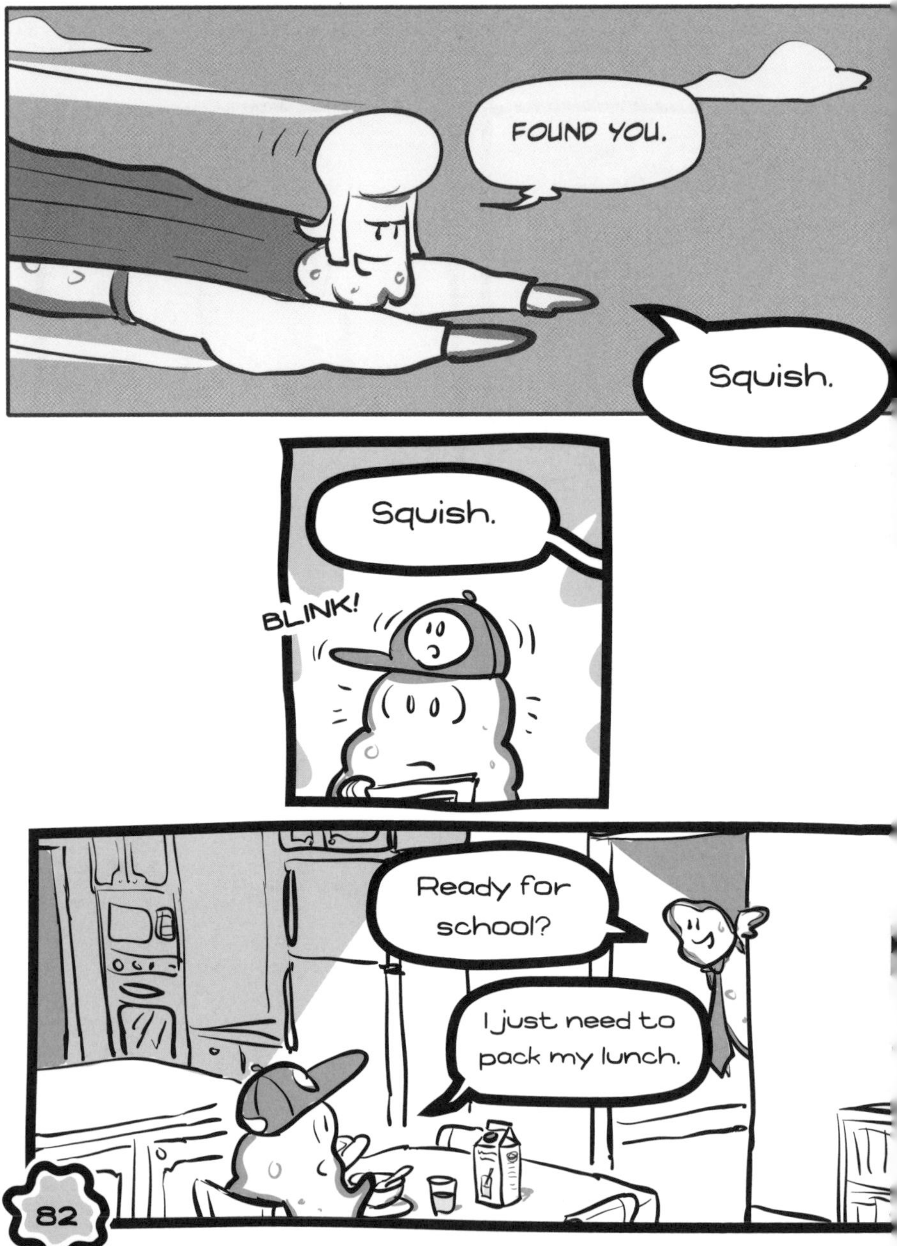
FOUND YOU.
Squish.
Squish.
BLINK!
Ready for school?
I just need to pack my lunch.

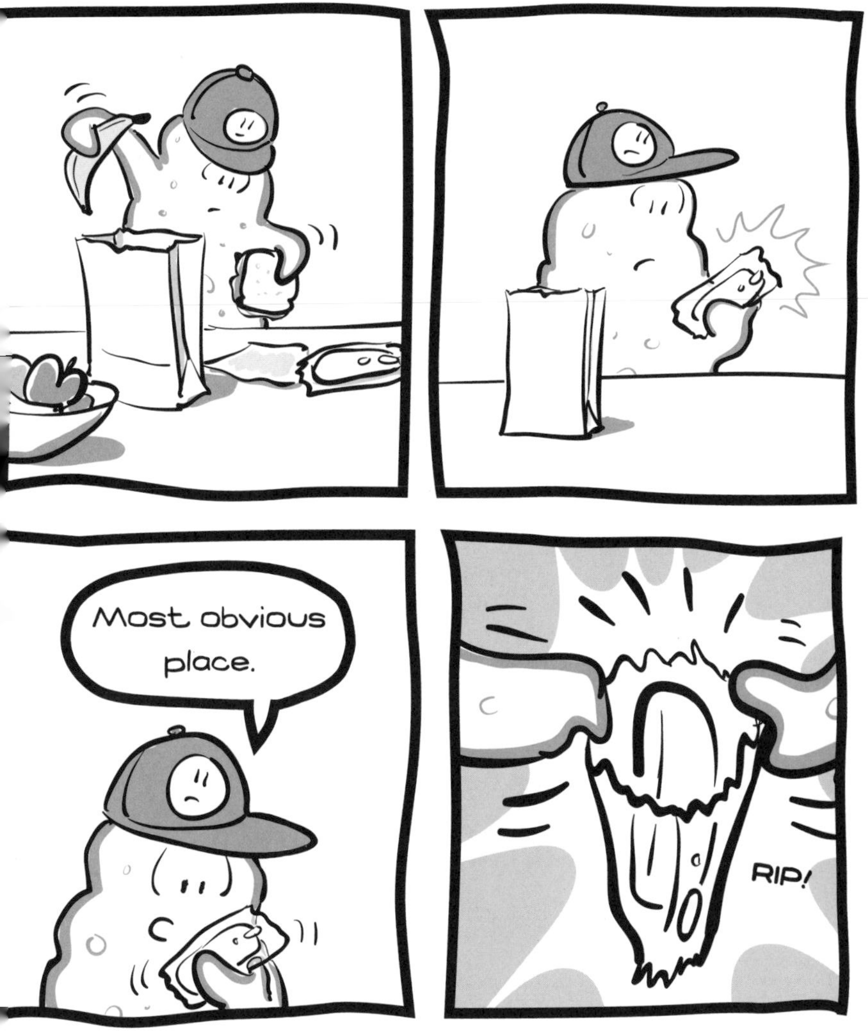
Most obvious place.
RIP!

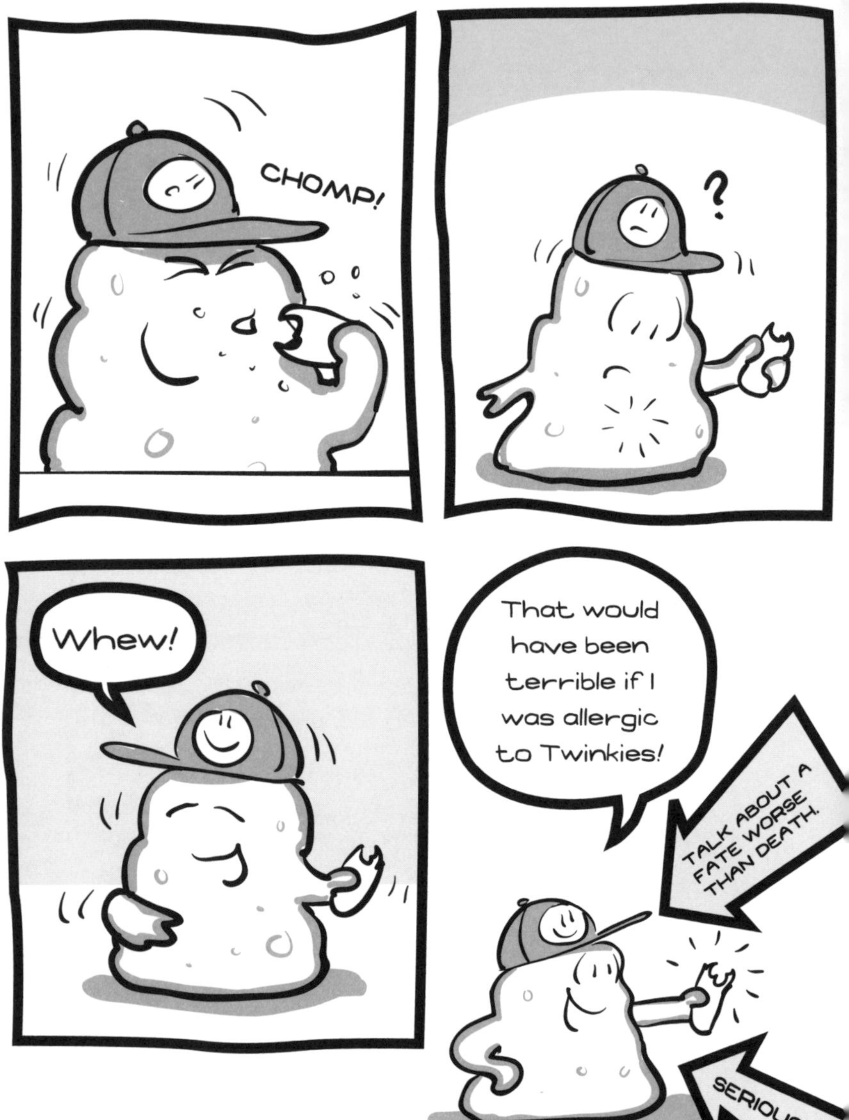
CHOMP!
?
Whew!
That would have been terrible if I was allergic to Twinkies!
TALK ABOUT A FATE WORSE THAN DEATH.
SERIOUSLY.

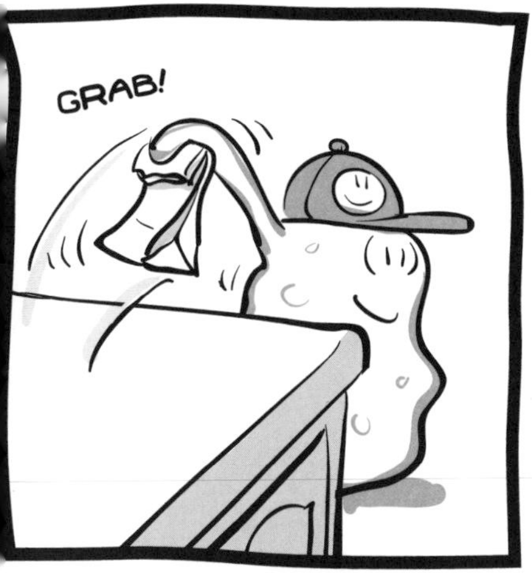
GRAB!

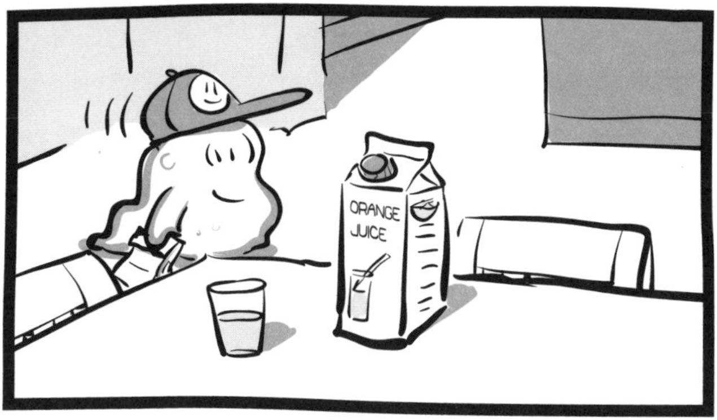
ORANGE
JUICE

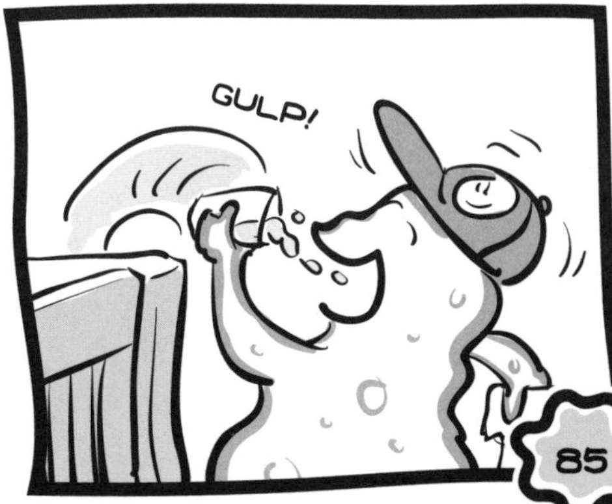
GULP!

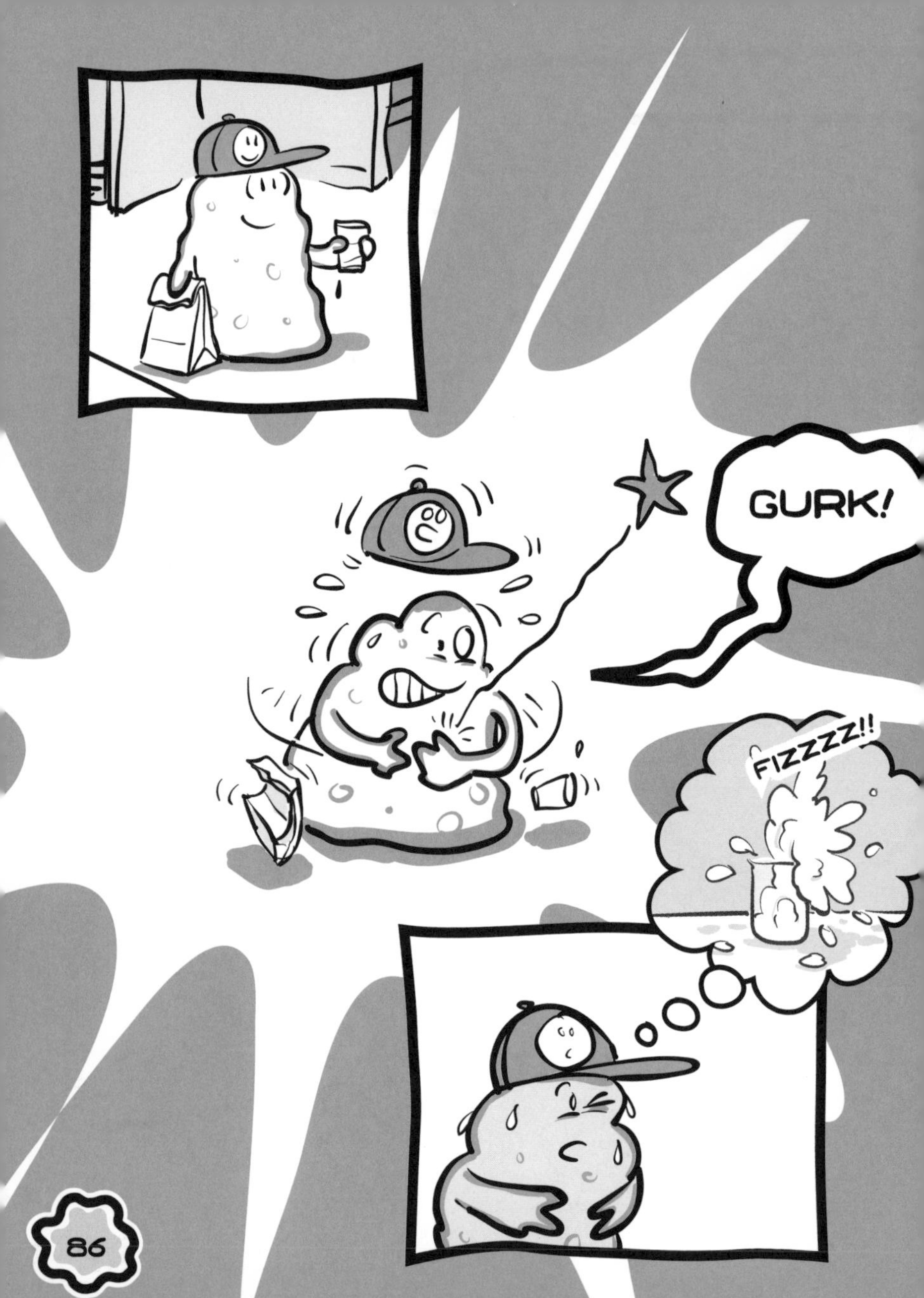
GURK!
FIZZZZ!!

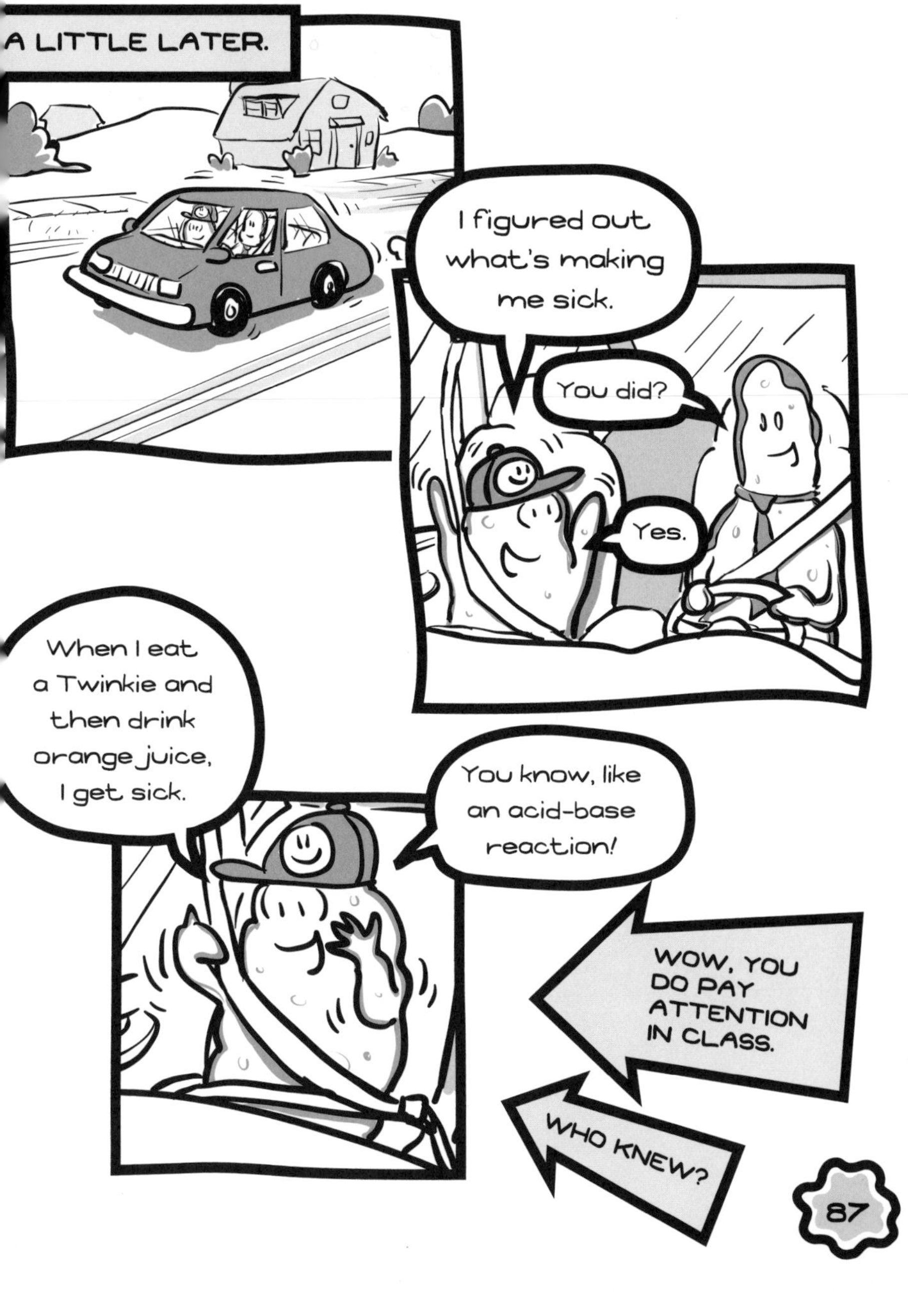
A LITTLE LATER.
I figured out what's making me sick.
You did?
Yes.
When I eat a Twinkie and then drink orange juice, I get sick.
You know, like an acid-base reaction!
WOW, YOU DO PAY ATTENTION IN CLASS.
WHO KNEW?

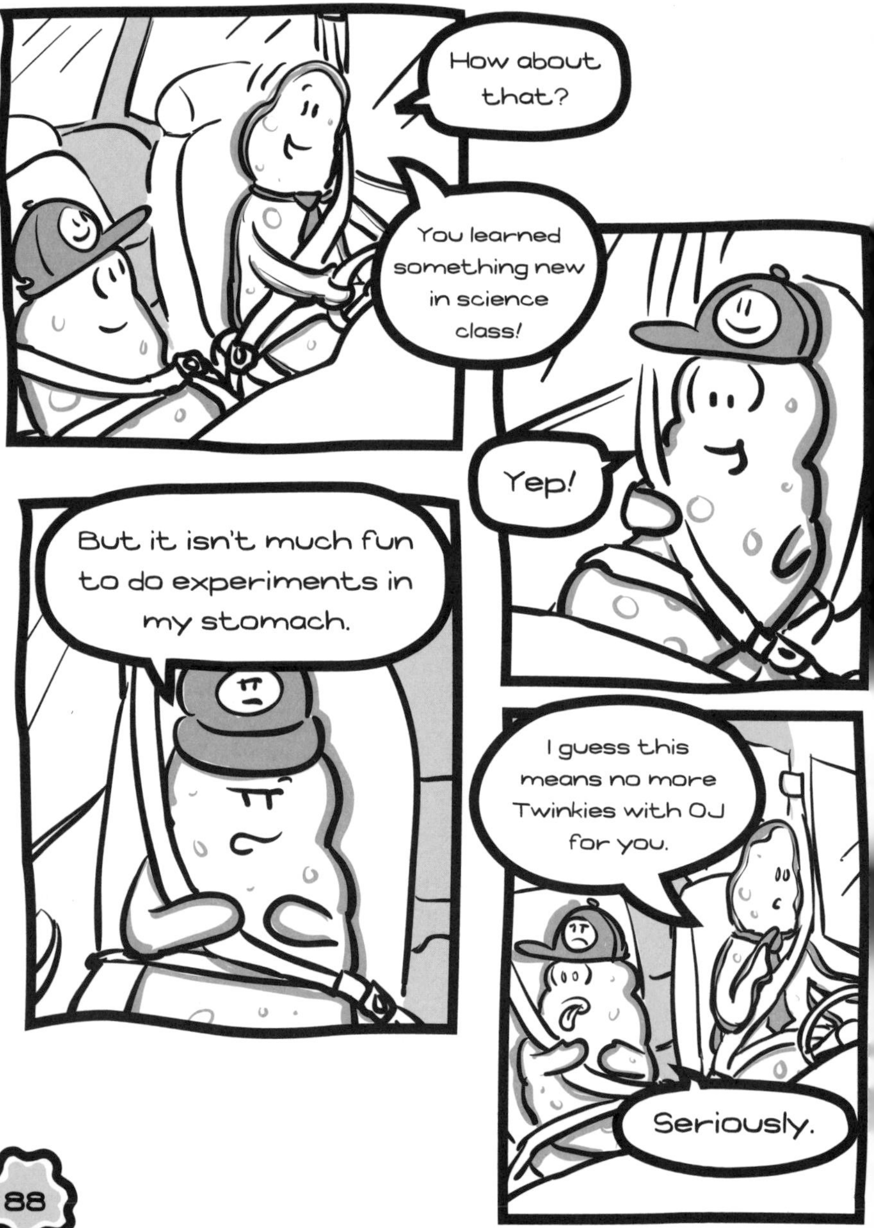
How about that?
You learned something new in science class!
Yep!
But it isn't much fun to do experiments in my stomach.
I guess this means no more Twinkies with OJ for you.
Seriously.

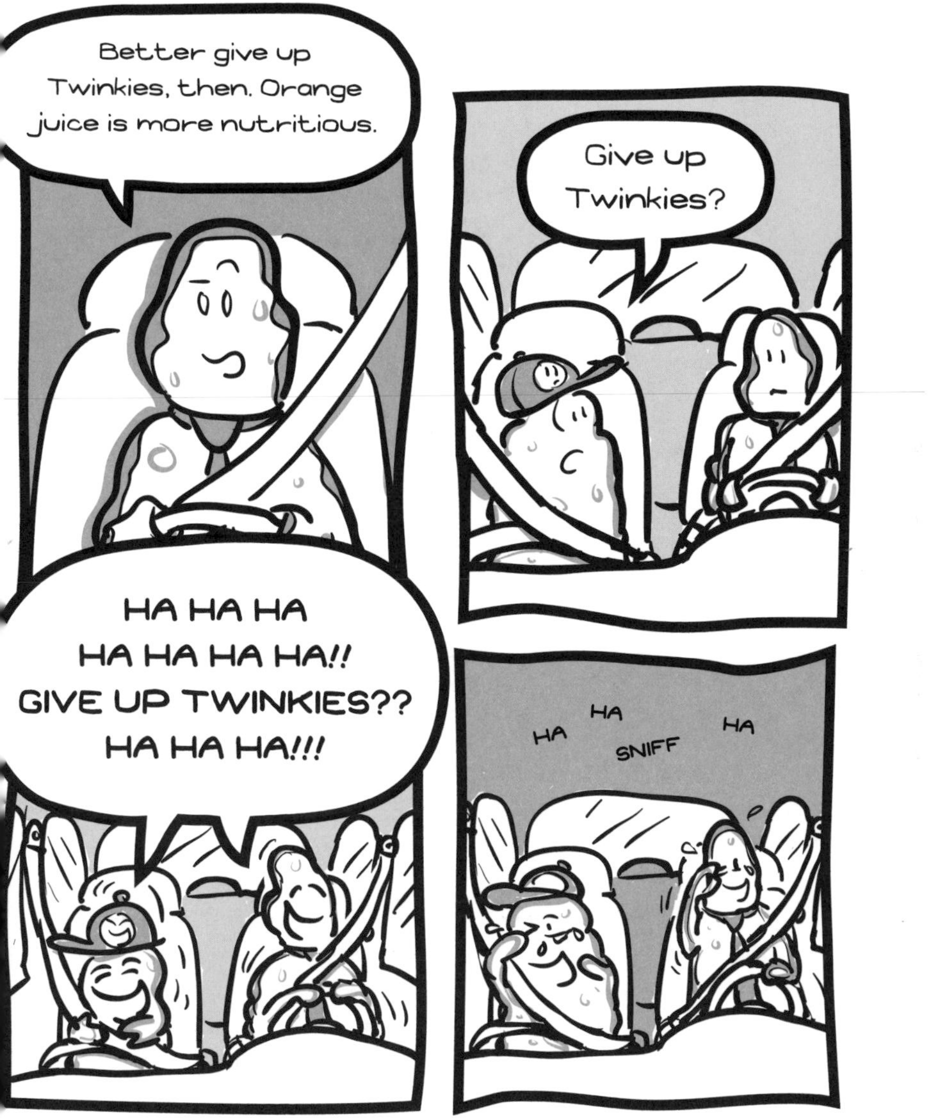
Better give up Twinkies, then. Orange juice is more nutritious.
Give up Twinkies?
HA HA HA HA HA HA HA!! GIVE UP TWINKIES?? HA HA HA!!!
HA
HA
HA
SNIFF

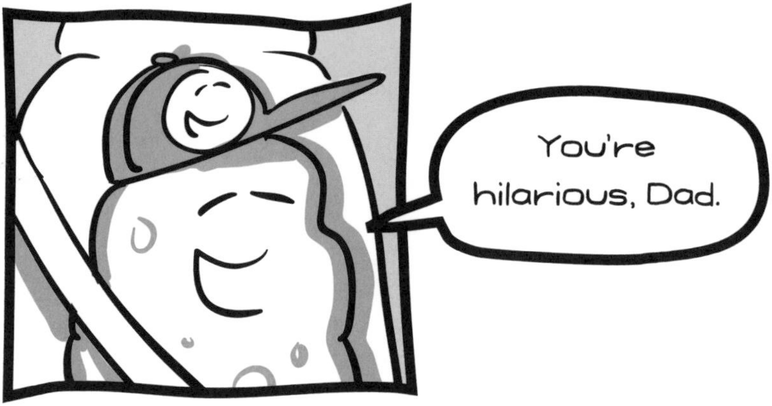

You're hilarious, Dad.

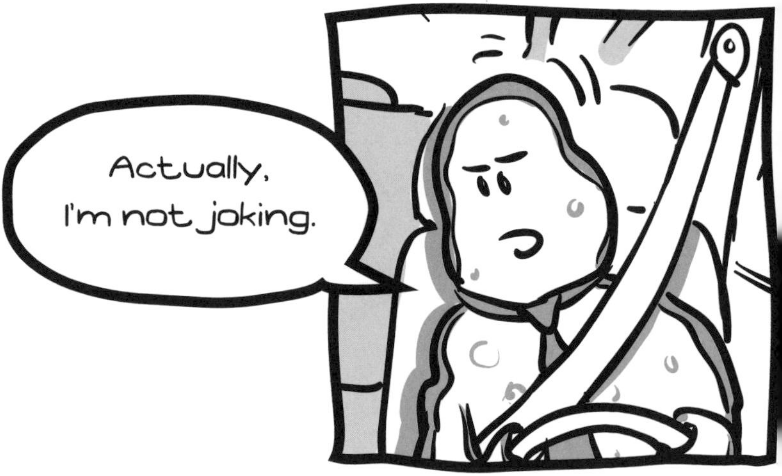

Actually, I'm not joking.

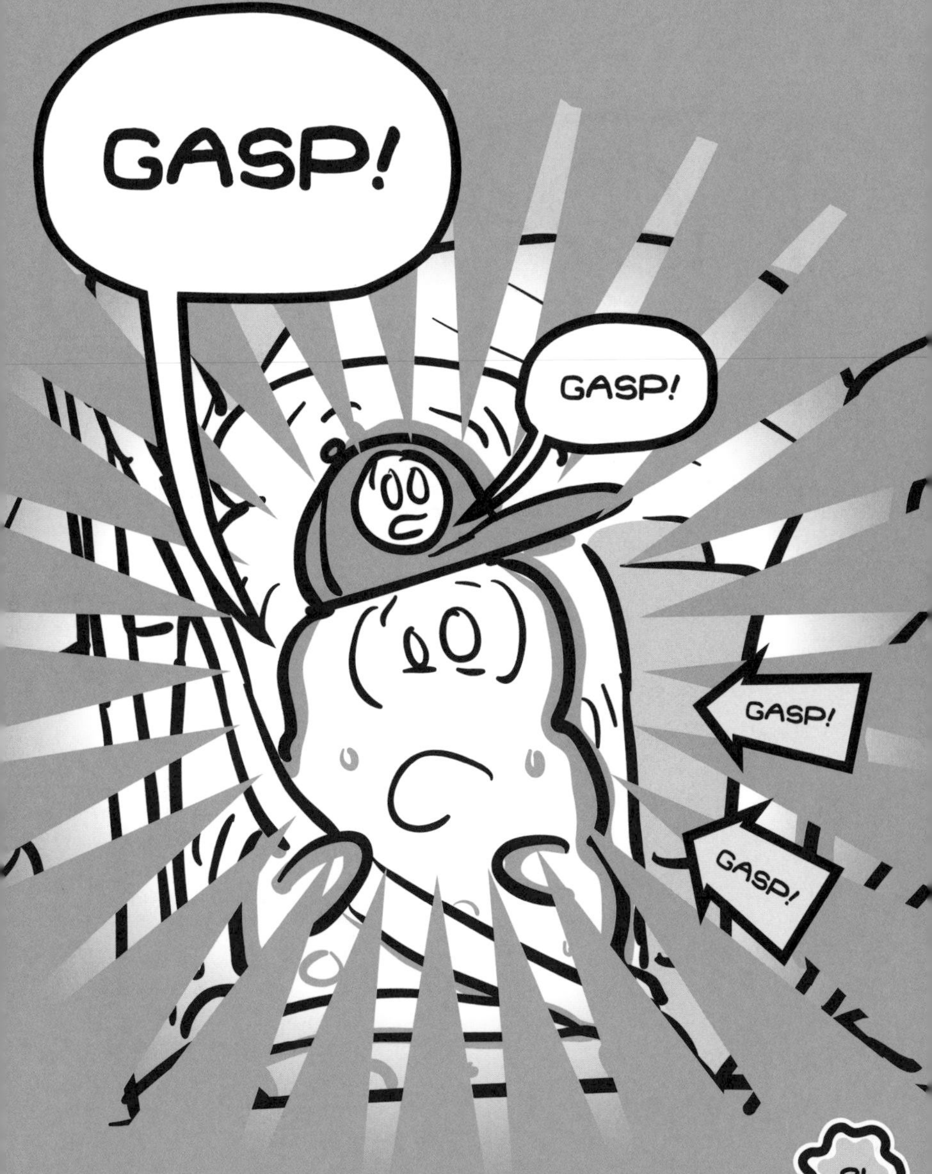
GASP!
GASP!
GASP!
GASP!

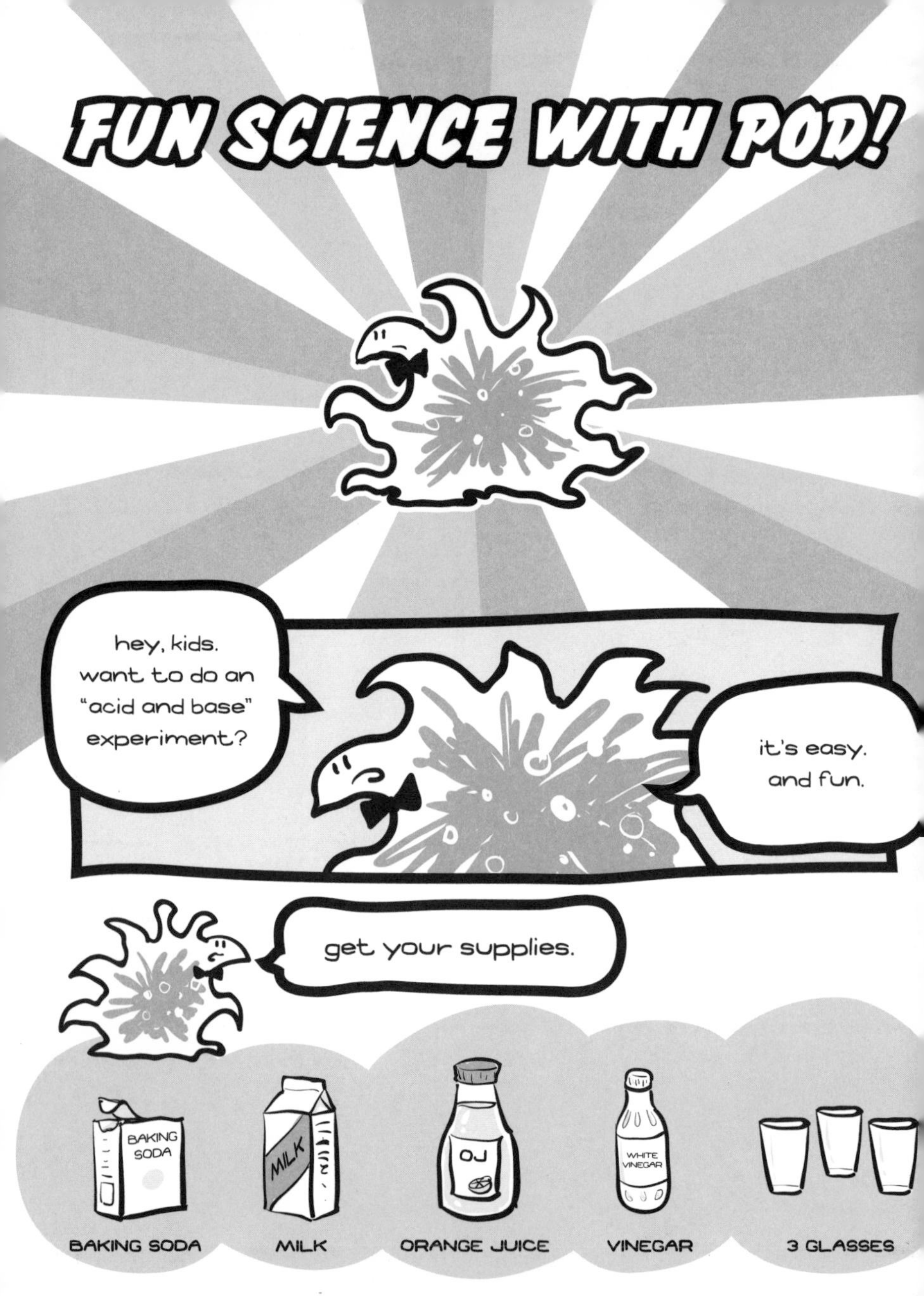
FUN SCIENCE WITH POD!
hey, kids. want to do an "acid and base" experiment?
it's easy. and fun.
get your supplies.
BAKING SODA
MILK
OJ
WHITE VINEGAR
BAKING SODA
MILK
ORANGE JUICE
VINEGAR
3 GLASSES

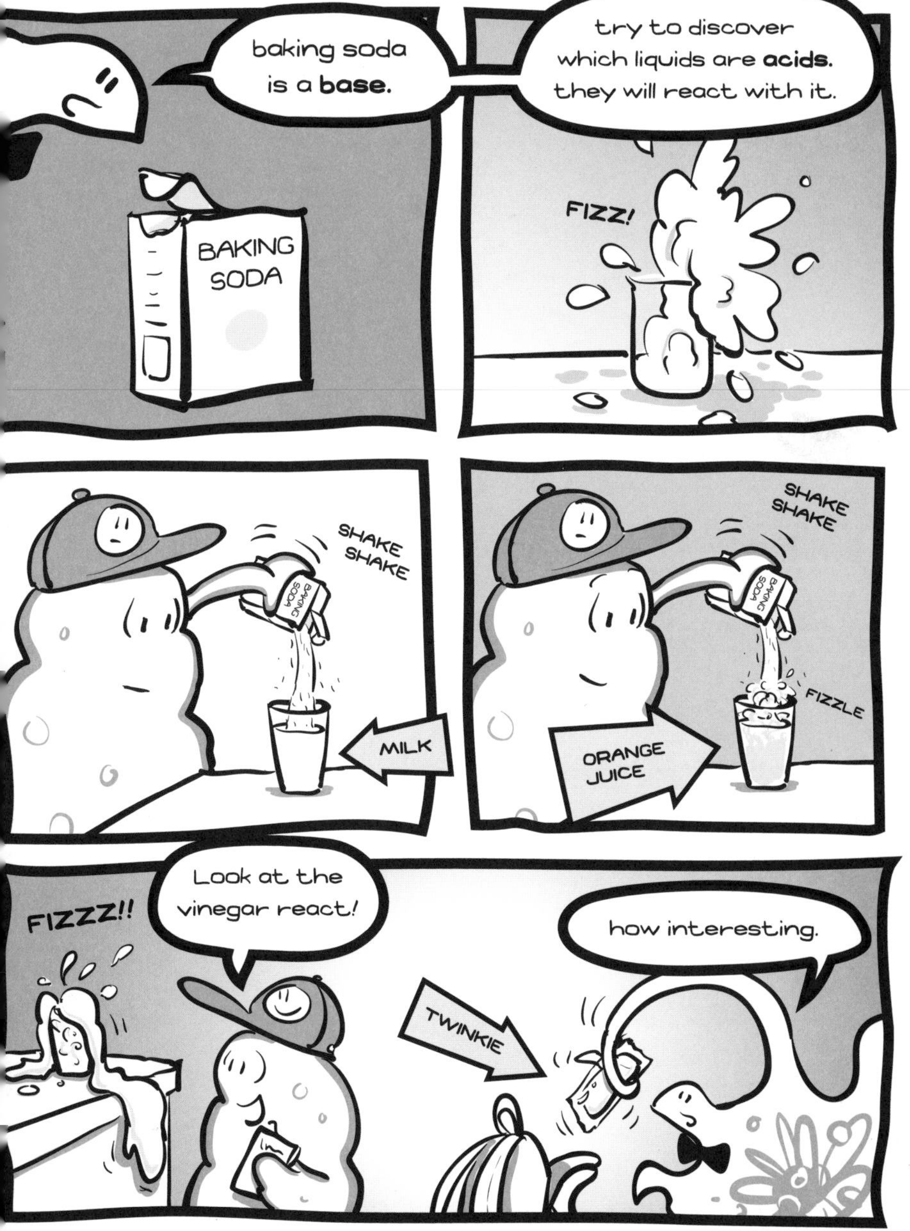
baking soda is a **base.**
BAKING SODA
try to discover which liquids are **acids.** they will react with it.
FIZZ!
SHAKE SHAKE
BAKING SODA
MILK
SHAKE SHAKE
BAKING SODA
FIZZLE
ORANGE JUICE
FIZZZ!!
Look at the vinegar react!
TWINKIE
how interesting.

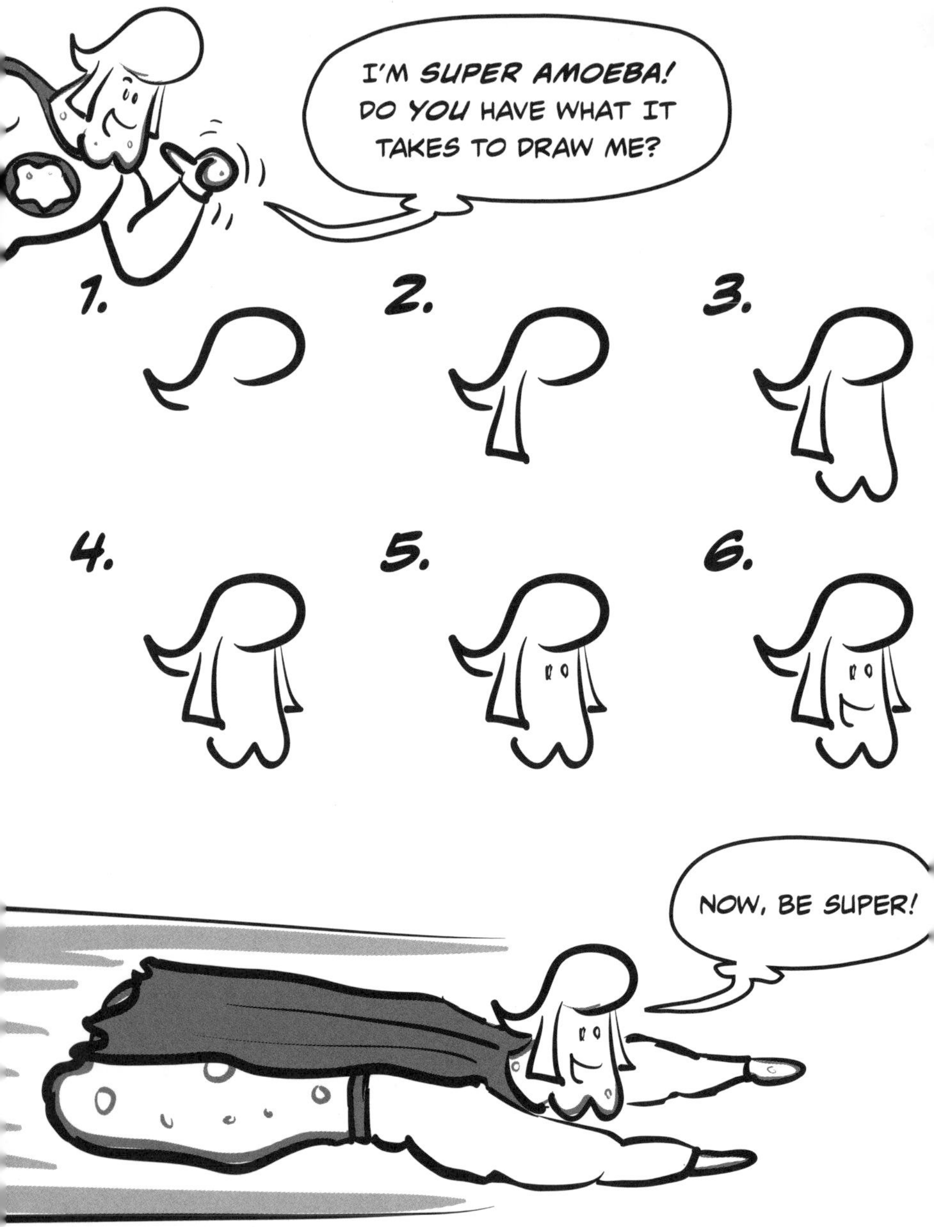

I'M SUPER AMOEBA! DO YOU HAVE WHAT IT TAKES TO DRAW ME?
1.
2.
3.
4.
5.
6.
NOW, BE SUPER!

IF YOU LIKE SQUISH, YOU'LL LOVE BABYMOUSE!

#1 BABYMOUSE: Queen of the World!
#2 BABYMOUSE: Our Hero
#3 BABYMOUSE: Beach Babe
#4 BABYMOUSE: Rock Star
#5 BABYMOUSE: Heartbreaker
#6 CAMP BABYMOUSE
#7 BABYMOUSE: Skater Girl
#8 BABYMOUSE: Puppy Love
#9 BABYMOUSE: Monster Mash
#10 BABYMOUSE: The Musical
#11 BABYMOUSE: Dragonslayer
#12 BABYMOUSE: Burns Rubber
#13 BABYMOUSE: Cupcake Tycoon
#14 BABYMOUSE: Mad Scientist
#15 A Very BABYMOUSE Christmas
#16 BABYMOUSE for President
#17 Extreme BABYMOUSE
#18 Happy Birthday, BABYMOUSE
#19 BABYMOUSE: Bad Babysitter

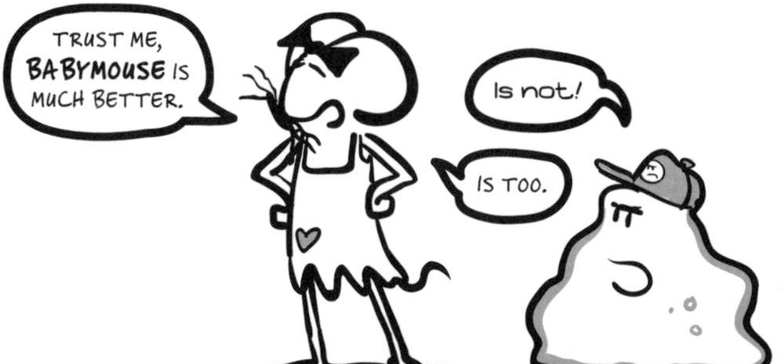
TRUST ME, BABYMOUSE IS MUCH BETTER.
Is not!
IS TOO.